KU-483-399

THE TANGO SINGER

BY THE SAME AUTHOR

Santa Evita

The Perón Novel

THE
TANGO SINGER

Tomás Eloy Martínez

Translated from the Spanish by Anne McLean

BLOOMSBURY

First published in Great Britain 2006
This paperback edition published 2007

Originally published by Planeta Argentina, 2004
Copyright © by Tomás Eloy Martínez 2004
English translation copyright © by Anne McLean 2006

The moral right of the author and translator has been asserted

Bloomsbury Publishing Plc, 36 Soho Square, London W1D 3QY

A CIP catalogue record for this book
is available from the British Library

ISBN 978 0 7475 8578 7

10 9 8 7 6 5 4 3 2

Typeset by Hewer Text UK Ltd, Edinburgh
Printed in Great Britain by Clays Limited, St Ives plc

All papers used by Bloomsbury Publishing are natural,
recyclable products made from wood grown in well-managed
forests. The manufacturing processes conform to the
environmental regulations of the country of origin

www.bloomsbury.com/tomaseloymartinez

For Sol Ana, who has fallen back in love
with Buenos Aires

For Gabriela Esquivada, without whom
this book would not exist

. . . an echo repeated through a thousand labyrinths

BAUDELAIRE *Les fleurs du mal*

Knowledge comes only in lightning flashes.
The text is the long roll of thunder that follows.

WALTER BENJAMIN *The Arcades Project*

ONE

September 2001

Buenos Aires was a city I knew only from literature until one mild winter's day in 2000 when I first heard the name Julio Martel. I'd recently passed my doctoral exams in literature at New York University and was writing a dissertation on Jorge Luis Borges' essays on the origins of the tango. The work was slow and confusing. I was tormented by the feeling I was just filling page after futile page. I spent hours staring out the window at neighboring houses on the Bowery as my life drifted away from me without my having the slightest idea what to do to catch up with it. I'd already missed too much of life and couldn't even console myself with the thought that something or someone else had taken it from me.

One of my professors had recommended I travel to Buenos Aires, but I didn't think it was necessary. I'd seen hundreds of photographs and films. I could imagine the humidity, the Río de la Plata, the drizzle, Borges tottering along the southern streets with his white cane. I had a collection of maps and Baedeker guides published in the same years as his books. I imagined a city much like Kuala

Lumpur: tropical and exotic, falsely modern, inhabited by descendants of Europeans who'd grown used to barbarism.

At midday, I decided to go for a wander around the Village. There were crowds of young guys in Tower Records on Broadway but I didn't stop this time. *Save your lips lest I return*, I mentally quoted Cernuda to them. *Farewell sweet, invisible lovers / I'm sorry I've not slept in your arms*.

As I passed the university bookstore I remembered I'd been meaning to buy a copy of Walter Benjamin's travel diaries for ages. I'd read it in the library and come away with an urge to underline passages and scribble in the margins. What could those distant notes, describing Moscow in 1926, Berlin in 1900, tell me about Buenos Aires? 'Don't worry if you can't get your bearings in a city' – that was one sentence I wanted to highlight in yellow.

Benjamin's books are usually shelved under Literary Criticism. For some reason they'd been moved to the Philosophy section at the opposite end of the store next to the Women's Studies aisles. As I made a beeline in that direction I came across Jean Franco crouched down examining a book about Mexican nuns. People will say that none of this is important, and the truth is it isn't, but I'd rather not overlook the slightest detail. Everyone knows Jean and there's no need to repeat who she is. I think she knew Borges was going to be Borges before he did. Forty years ago she discovered the new Latin American novel when only specialists in Naturalism and Regionalism were interested. I'd only visited her a couple of times in her apartment on Manhattan's Upper West Side, but she greeted me as if we saw each other every day. I started describing the general outline of my thesis and I must have gotten in a muddle. I can't remember how long I spent trying to explain that, for Borges, the only true tangos were those composed before 1910, when they were still danced in brothels, and not the ones that appeared later, influenced by Parisian tastes and Genoese tarantellas. Jean undoubtedly knew more about the matter than I did, because she brought up some obscene songs no one remembered any more: *I'm a Big Shot, Ramrod, Whatcha Got Up There, Won't Let Me In*, and *Bangin'*.

In Buenos Aires, she told me, there's this extraordinary guy who sings very old tangos. Not those ones exactly, but there is a family resemblance. You should hear him.

Maybe I could find something at Tower Records, I said. What's his name?

Julio Martel. But you won't, because he's never recorded a single line. He doesn't like any mediation between his voice and his audience. One night, when some friends took me to the Club del Vino, he limped onto the stage and leaned on a stool. He can't walk very well – there's something wrong with his legs. The guitarist who accompanied him played first, on his own . . . a very strange, weary music. When we least expected it, he unleashed his voice. It was incredible. I was floating in mid-air, and when the voice fell silent, I didn't know how to detach myself from it, how to get back to earth. You know how much I love opera, how I adore Raimondi and Callas, but the Martel experience is like another dimension, almost supernatural.

Like Gardel, I ventured.

You've got to hear him. He's better than Gardel.

The image kept going around in my head and eventually turned into an obsession. For months I could think of nothing but traveling to Buenos Aires to hear the singer. I read everything I could find about the city on the internet. I knew what was playing at the cinemas and theaters. I knew the temperature every day. The notion of the seasons being reversed from one hemisphere to the other disturbed me. The leaves were falling there and in New York I was watching them come to life.

At the end of May 2001, the graduate school awarded me a grant. I also won a Fulbright scholarship. I could live on that money for six months, if not longer. Although Buenos Aires was an expensive city, the banks paid interest rates of 9 to 12 per cent on deposit accounts. I figured I'd have enough to rent a furnished downtown apartment and buy books.

I'd been told the trip to the far south of the continent was long, but mine was madness. I was in the air for more than fourteen hours, and, with stops in Miami and Santiago de Chile, it took twenty altogether. I landed at Ezeiza airport exhausted. The space for passport control was taken up by a luxurious duty-free shop, forcing the passengers to line up, all packed together, under a staircase. When I finally got through customs I was besieged by six or seven taxi drivers offering to take me into the city. I got away from them with great difficulty. After changing my dollars for pesos – they were at par back then – I called the *pensión* recommended by the international office of the university. The concierge kept me on hold for ages before telling me my name didn't appear on any list and the *pensión* was full. Call back next week, buddy. You might be in luck, he said as he hung up, with an insolent familiarity that, I soon found out, was how everyone talked.

Behind me, in the line of people waiting for the phone, there was a gawky, gloomy-looking youth, intently biting his nails. It was a pity, because his long, tapered fingers turned graceless at their stubby ends. His biceps barely fit inside his rolled-up shirtsleeves. I couldn't keep from noticing his eyes, black and moist like Omar Sharif's.

They're fucking you around. You got skanked, he said to me. It happens all the time. Everything's a racket in this country.

I couldn't think what to answer. The language he was speaking was not the one I knew. His accent had none of the Italian cadences of Argentine Spanish. He aspirated his s's. His r's didn't reverberate on the roof of his mouth, but escaped through clenched teeth. I stepped back from the telephone so he could use it, but he gave up his place in line and followed me. The information office was ten feet away and I figured they'd know of other hotels for the same price.

If you're looking for somewhere to stay, I can get you the best deal, he said. Lots of light, overlooking the street, four hundred a month. They change your sheets and towels once a week. You've got to share a bathroom, but it's nice and clean. What d'you say?

I don't know, I said. Really, I wanted to say no.

7

I can talk them down to three hundred.

Where is it? I asked, unfolding the map I'd bought at the Rand McNally bookstore. I decided to object to whichever area he pointed to.

You gotta understand it's not a hotel. It's a bit more private. A boarding house, in a historic building. On Garay between Bolívar and Defensa.

Garay was the street in 'The Aleph,' the Borges short story I'd written an essay on in the last year of my masters. But, according to the map, this *pensión* was about five blocks from the house described in the story.

The aleph, I said involuntarily. It seemed impossible he would understand this reference, but the guy caught it in mid-air.

That's the one. How'd you know? Once a month, a municipal bus brings tourists, shows them the boarding house from the outside and tells them: 'This is the house of the Alé.' As far as I know there was never any famous Alé who lived there, so maybe they're having them on. But don't go thinking they're any hassle, eh? Everything's cool. They take their photos, climb back on their bus, and bye-bye.

I'd like to see the house, I said. And the room. Maybe they could put a desk by the window.

The guy's nose curved like a falcon's beak. It was thinner than a falcon's and didn't look too bad on him; anyway his fleshy mouth and big eyes were more prominent features. In the taxi he told me his life story, but I barely paid attention. I was stupid with exhaustion from the long trip and I couldn't believe my good luck was taking me straight to the house from 'The Aleph.' I half understood his name, which was Omar or Oscar. But he was from Tucumán and everyone, he said, called him El Tucumano.

I also found out he worked at a magazine kiosk in the airport, sometimes for three hours, sometimes ten, never the same workday.

I came to work without having slept today, he said. What's the point, ya know?

On both sides of the highway leading into the city, the landscape changed from one moment to the next. A still, soft mist hovered over the fields, but the sky was clear and sweet scents wafted through the air. I saw a Mormon temple, its tower topped by an image of the angel Moroni; I saw tall, ugly buildings with lines of colored washing hanging out the windows, like in Italy; I saw a ravine filled with miserable shacks, which might collapse at the first gust of wind. Then came the imitation European suburbs: deserted parks, tower blocks like aviaries, churches with bell towers crowned with statues of the Virgin Mary, houses with huge satellite dishes on their roof terraces. Buenos Aires didn't look like Kuala Lumpur. In fact, it looked like almost every place I'd ever seen; meaning, it didn't look like anywhere else.

What do they call you? El Tucumano asked.

Bruno, I said. Bruno Cadogan.

Cadogan? Not much luck with your surname there, buddy. Spin around the last two syllables and it means 'shitting' in this neck of the woods.

The woman at the reception in the boarding house wrote down Cagan, or 'they shit,' and when she took me upstairs to see the room she called me 'Mister Cagan.' I ended up begging her to just call me by my first name.

I was surprised by the decrepit state of the house. Nothing there recalled the middle-class family Borges described in his story. The location was also disconcerting. All the references to the aleph's whereabouts mention Garay Street, near the corner of Bernardo de Irigoyen, to the west of the boarding house. But still I asked whether the house had a cellar. Yes, the manager told me, but it's taken. You wouldn't want to live there, sir. It's very damp and besides, there are nineteen very steep steps. This piece of information took me aback. In the short story the steps leading down to the aleph also numbered nineteen.

All Buenos Aires was new to me so I had nothing to compare to the room on offer. I thought it seemed small, about eight feet by ten, but clean. On one side of the foam-rubber mattress, which was on a wooden frame, there was a tiny table with room for my laptop. The best thing about the place were some old library shelves, with space for about fifty books. The sheets were threadbare and the blanket must have pre-dated the house. The room had a small balcony overlooking the street. I later found out it was the biggest room on the top floor. Although the bathroom looked minuscule, I'd only have to share it with the family next door.

I had to pay in advance. The rate posted by the reception counter read four hundred dollars a month.

El Tucumano, true to his word, got Enriqueta to accept three.

It was four in the afternoon. The place was empty and peaceful and I was ready for a sleep. El Tucumano had been renting a room on the roof terrace for the last six months. He was dead tired as well, he told me. We arranged to meet at eight to go wander around the city. If I'd had any strength, I would have gone out then and there to look for Julio Martel. But I didn't know where to start, or how.

At seven I was startled awake by an uproar. My next-door neighbors were screaming at each other. I got dressed as best I could and tried to go into the bathroom. A huge woman was washing clothes in the bidet and told me, rudely, to hang on. When I went downstairs, El Tucumano was by the reception desk sipping *maté* with Enriqueta.

I don't know what to do about those animals, said the manager. One of these days they're going to kill each other. I wish I'd never let them have a room. I'd no idea they were from Fuerte Apache.

I thought *Fort Apache* was a John Ford movie. From Enriqueta's tone of voice it sounded like she was summoning up some pit of hell.

Have a wash in my bathroom if you want, Cagan, said El Tucumano. I'm going to the *milongas* at eleven. We'll get something to eat on the way and then, if you feel like it, I'll take you.

That evening, ten days before the Twin Towers were destroyed, I saw Buenos Aires for the first time. At seven-thirty an other-worldly pink light fell on the façades of the buildings. Despite El Tucumano's insistence that the city was in ruins and that I should have seen it a year ago, when its beauty was still intact and there weren't so many beggars on the streets, I saw only happy people. We walked down an enormous avenue, lined with flowering jacarandas. Every time I looked up I discovered baroque palaces and cupolas in the shape of parasols or melons, with purely ornamental turrets. I was surprised that Buenos Aires was so majestic from the second or third story upwards and so dilapidated at street level, as if the splendor of the past had remained suspended in the heights and refused to descend or disappear. As the night wore on, the cafés became ever fuller. I'd never seen so many in a single city, and all so hospitable. The majority of the clients sat there reading with an empty cup on the table for ages – we passed the same places several times – without being asked to pay up and leave, as would have happened in New York or Paris. I thought those cafés were perfect for writing novels. Reality didn't know what to do there and wandered around loose, hunting for authors who would dare to tell it. Everything seemed very real, perhaps too real, although I didn't see it like that then. I didn't understand why Argentines preferred to write fantastic or unbelievable stories about lost civilizations or human clones or holograms on desert islands when reality was so intense you could feel it burning up, and burning, stinging your skin.

We walked for ages and nothing seemed to be where it belonged. The cinema where Juan Perón had met his first wife, on Santa Fe Avenue, was now a record and video store. In some of the box seats there were artificial flowers; in others, big empty shelves. We ate pizza in a place that looked like a haberdashery and still had buttons, edging and lace in the window. El Tucumano told me the best place to learn tangos wasn't the Academia Gaeta, as the tourist guides all said, but a bookstore called El Rufián Melancólico or the Melancholy Pimp. I'd found out from the internet that Martel had sung there for a while after they rescued him from a humble trattoria in Boedo, where his only pay had been tips and a free meal. El Tucumano thought it strange he'd never heard that story, especially in a city abounding in experts on all sorts of music – from rock and shanty-town *cumbias* to bossa nova and John Cage sonatas – but especially in tango experts, able to distinguish the subtlest nuance between a 1958 quintet and one from 1962. For him not to have heard of Martel was ridiculous. For a moment I thought he might not exist, maybe Jean Franco had merely dreamed him.

On the top floor of El Rufián there was a dance practice going on. The women had slim waists and understanding eyes, and the guys, though they wore their sleepless nights on their worn-out sleeves, moved with a marvelous delicacy and corrected partners' errors by whispering in their ears. Downstairs, the bookstore was full of people, like almost every bookstore we'd seen. Thirty years earlier, Julio Cortázar and Gabriel García Márquez had been surprised that Buenos Aires housewives would buy *Hopscotch* and *One Hundred Years of Solitude* as if they were noodles or lettuce and take the books home in their grocery bags. I noticed that *porteños* still read as avidly as they had back then. Their habits, however, had changed. They didn't buy books any more. They'd begin a book in one shop and continue reading it in another, ten pages in one, ten pages in the next, or a chapter in each, until they finished it. They'd spend days or weeks on a single book.

The owner of El Rufián, Mario Virgili, was at the bar on the top floor when we arrived. While keeping an eye on everything that was going on, he moved outside of events, looking both contemplative and agitated. I'd never imagined those two qualities could blend in the same person. When I sat down beside him nothing seemed to move but I could tell that everything was in motion. I heard my friend call him Tano and I also heard him ask if I planned on staying in Buenos Aires for very long. I answered that I wouldn't leave until I'd found Julio Martel, but his attention was already elsewhere.

One dance finished and the couples separated as if they had nothing to do with each other. I'd found that ritual disconcerting when I saw it in films, but in reality it was stranger still. Between one tango and the next, a man would invite a woman to dance with a nod that seemed indifferent. It wasn't. The disdain was feigned to protect their pride from any slight. If the woman accepted, she would do so with a distant smile and stand up, so the man would come over to her. When the music began, the couple would stand waiting for some seconds, one in front of the other, making small talk without looking at each other. Then the dance began with a somewhat brutal embrace. The man's arm encircled the woman's waist and from that moment she began to back away. She was always on the retreat. Sometimes, he arched his chest forward or turned sideways, cheek to cheek, while his legs sketched tangled figures that the woman would have to repeat in reverse. The dance demanded great precision and, most of all, a certain talent for divination, because the steps didn't follow a predictable order but were either up to the one who was leading to improvise or choreographed from infinite combinations. With couples who understood each other best, some of the dance's movements mimicked copulation. It looked like athletic sex, tending towards perfection but with no interest in love. I thought it would be useful to incorporate some of these observations into my doctoral thesis, because they confirmed the brothel origins Borges attributed to the tango in *Evaristo Carriego*.

One of the dance instructors came over and asked me if I'd like to try out a few figures.

Go on, give it a try, Tano said. Everyone learns with Valeria.

I hesitated. Valeria aroused an instinctive trust, a desire to protect her, and tenderness. Her face resembled my maternal grandmother's. She had a clear, high forehead and almond-shaped brown eyes.

I'm very clumsy, I said. Don't make me embarrass myself.

Okay then, I'll come and find you later.

Later, another time, I answered and meant it.

Each time Tano Virgili got up from his barstool to

observe the couples coming and going across the floor, I was left open-mouthed with something halfway uttered. The word would drop off my lips and roll out between the dancers, who would crush it under their heels before I could pick it up. Finally I managed to get him to answer my question about Julio Martel in such detail that when I got back to the boarding house I had trouble summarizing. 'Martel,' he told me, 'was actually called Estéfano Caccace. He changed it because with a name like that no one would ever have been able to give him a serious introduction. Imagine: Caccace. He sang here, near where you're sitting, and there was a time when people in the know spoke of nothing but his voice, which was unique. Perhaps it still is. I haven't heard anything of him for ages.' He put a hand on my shoulder and came out with the predictable acclaim: 'If you ask me, he was better than Gardel. But don't repeat that.'

After that night I took a swarm of notes that might perhaps be faithful to Virgili's tale, but I've a feeling I've lost the tone, the atmosphere of what he said.

I barely remember the long walk El Tucumano and I took later. We went from one part of the city to another, on what he called 'the *milonga* pilgrimage.' Despite the scenery and cast changing at a pace my senses couldn't keep up with – going from pitch dark to psychedelic lights, from dance halls for men to others where they projected images of a past and perhaps illusory Buenos Aires, with avenues that echoed those of Madrid, Paris and Milan, from retired violin trios to orchestras of young ladies – my spirit had stopped at some point where nothing was happening, like dawn on the morning of a battle that was about to break out elsewhere, perhaps due to the fatigue of the trip or because I expected the intangible Martel might appear at any point during the endless night. We went to the vast warehouse of El Parakultural, and to El Catedral, to La Viruta and El Beso, which were almost empty because the *milonga* ritual changed according to the day. There were places for dancing between one and three in the morning on Wednesdays, or Fridays from eleven to four. The spiderweb of names added confusion to the liturgy. I heard a couple of German aficionados would arrange to meet in the Parakultural calling it the Sociedad Helénica, although I later found out that this was just the name of the building, located on a street that for some was called Canning and for others Scalabrini Ortiz. That night I had the impression that Martel could be in two or three places at once, or in none. I also thought he might not exist at all and was just one more of the city's many fables. Borges had said, quoting Bishop Berkeley, that if no one perceived something, that thing had no reason to exist, *esse est percipi*. For a moment I felt the phrase could define the whole city.

Around three in the morning I saw Valeria again in a huge hall called La Estrella, which the previous Saturday had been called La Viruta. She was dancing with a Japanese tourist who was dressed in tango attire straight out of a manual: gleaming shoes with heels, tight pants, a double-breasted jacket that he unbuttoned when the music stopped, and a brilliantined sculpture on top of his head that looked as if it had been drawn on with a ruler and compass. I was struck by how Valeria looked just as fresh as she had five hours earlier, in El Rufián, and how she led the Japanese man with the dexterity of a puppeteer, obliging him to spin on his own axis and cross his feet over and over again, while she remained still on the dance floor, concentrated on her body's center of gravity.

I think that was the last vision I retained of the night because the only other thing I remember is being on a late bus, getting out near the boarding house on Garay Street and throwing myself onto the blessed darkness of my bed.

I read in an old issue of *Satiricón* that Julio Martel's real mother, ashamed that her newborn baby resembled an insect, put him in a wicker basket and threw him into the waters of the Riachuelo, where his adoptive parents rescued him. That tale always seemed to me a religious diversion from the truth. I tend to believe the version Tano Virgili told me is more accurate.

Martel was born towards the end of the torrid summer of 1945, on a number 96 streetcar, which in those days ran between Villa Urquiza and the Plaza de Mayo. At about three in the afternoon, Señora Olivia de Caccace, seven months pregnant and short of breath, was walking along Donado Street. One of her sisters had the flu and she was on the way to her house, with a basket of poultices and a bag of fudge pieces in cellophane wrappers. The flagstones of the sidewalk were loose and Señora Olivia was walking very carefully. Along the whole length of the block, all the houses shared the same monotonous appearance: a pot-bellied, wrought-iron balcony on the right-hand side of a hallway giving onto an inner glass door with beveled edges and monograms. Beneath the balcony a grilled window opened, occasionally revealing the silhouette of a child or an old woman, for whom the landscape of the street, seen from ground level, was the sole entertainment. None of those houses now resemble what they were half a century ago. The majority of families, in the struggle to survive, must have been forced to sell off the glass of the doors and the iron of the balconies to building yards.

When Señora Olivia passed in front of the house at number 1620 Donado Street, a hand grabbed one of her ankles and threw her down to the ground. Later they found out that a mentally handicapped man in his late thirties lived there; he'd been left by the cellar window to get some fresh air. Attracted by a glimpse of the fudge, the imbecile could think of no better ruse than to trip the woman.

Hearing her cries for help, a well-meaning soul managed to get Señora Olivia seated in a number 96 streetcar, which was providentially stopped at the corner. There were several hospitals along that route, so the conductor was asked to drop her off at the nearest one. She didn't make it to any of them. Ten minutes into the journey, Señora Olivia felt herself losing a torrent of liquid and was suddenly in the last stages of labor. The vehicle stopped and the conductor desperately called up to the houses in the neighborhood for scissors and boiling water. The premature baby, a boy, needed to be put into an incubator. The mother insisted he be baptized as soon as possible with the name of his father who'd died six months earlier, Stéfano. Neither the parish nor the Civil Register would accept Italian spelling, so he was finally inscribed as Estéfano Esteban.

Although he was allergic to cats and pollen, suffered frequent bouts of diarrhea and headaches, the child grew normally up to the age of six. He loved playing soccer and seemed to have a gift for quick attacks from the wings. Every afternoon, while Señora Olivia toiled away at her sewing machine, Estéfano ran around the patio behind the ball, dodging imaginary opponents. On one of those occasions he tripped on a loose brick and fell. An enormous contusion immediately formed on his left leg. The pain was atrocious, but the incident seemed so trivial his mother didn't think it was significant. The next day the bruise had spread and turned a threatening purple.

At the hospital they diagnosed Estéfano as a hemophiliac. It took him a month to recover. When he got up, brushing against a chair caused another hemorrhage. They had to put him in a plaster cast. He was thus condemned to such constant stillness that his muscles wasted away. Since then – if there is such a thing as then for something endless – he's had continuous misfortune. The child developed a huge torso, out of proportion to his stunted legs. He couldn't go to school and saw only one friend, Mocho Andrade, who lent him books and resigned himself to playing innumerable games of cards. He learned to read fluently from private teachers who taught him as a favor. When he was eleven or twelve he'd spend hours listening to tangos on the radio and, when one interested him, he'd copy the lyrics down in a notebook. Sometimes, he wrote down the melodies, too. Since he couldn't read music, he invented a system of lines with dots of ten or twelve different colours and circumferences that enabled him to remember chords and rhythms.

The day one of Señora Olivia's clients brought him a copy of *20th Century Songbirds*, Estéfano was struck by an epiphany. The magazine contained tangos withdrawn from the repertoires at the beginning of the twentieth century, songs recounting the raunchy goings-on in brothels. Estéfano didn't know the meanings of the words he was reading. His mother and her clients were no help either, because the language of those tangos had been invented to allude to the intimate behavior of people who had died many years earlier. The sounds, however, were eloquent. Since the original scores had been lost, Estéfano imagined melodies that imitated the style of *El entrerriano (The Man from Entre Ríos)* or *La morocha (The Brunette)*, and applied them to lines like these: *As soon as I snap your snuggle / my blangle starts to blong / inside you've so much tuggle / that if I waloop, I'll walong.*

By the age of fifteen, he could repeat more than one hundred songs reciting them backwards, with the imaginary music reversed as well, but he only did it when his mother left the house to deliver her sewing work. He'd lock himself in the bathroom, where the neighbours couldn't hear him, and unleash an intense, sweet soprano voice. The beauty of his own singing moved him to such an extent that unnoticed tears would spill down his cheeks. He so scorned and mistrusted himself that he found it incredible this voice could belong to him, rather than to Carlos Gardel, to whom all voices belonged. He looked at his weedy body in the mirror and offered to God all that he was and all that he might one day become in exchange for a glimpse of the slightest gesture reminiscent of his idol. For hours he stood in front of the mirror, with his mother's white scarf wrapped around his neck, pronouncing a few phrases he'd heard the great singer say in his Hollywood movies: 'Ciao, chick-eeadee,' 'Look, what a luvally dawn.'

Estéfano had thick lips and curly, wiry hair. Any physical resemblance to Gardel was out of the question. He imitated the smile then, slightly twisting the corners of his lips and stretching the skin across his forehead, with his teeth shining brightly. 'Good morning, my good fellellow,' he'd say. 'How's life terreating you?'

By the time they removed the cast, when he was sixteen, his legs were stiff and weak. A physiotherapist helped him to strengthen the muscles in exchange for clothes for his entire family. Estéfano took six months to learn how to walk with crutches and a further six to learn how to get around with walking sticks, terrified at the thought of another fall and being laid up again for a prolonged period.

One Sunday in the summer, Señora Olivia and two friends took him to the funfair on Libertador Avenue. Since they wouldn't let him go on any of the rides, for fear he'd hurt himself or dislocate his fragile little bones, the adolescent was bored all afternoon, licking at the cotton candy Mocho Andrade bought for him. While he was waiting beside the ghost train tent, he discovered an electroacoustic kiosk where they recorded voices onto acetate discs for the modest sum of three pesos. Estéfano convinced the women to go around at least twice on the ghost train and, as soon as he saw them disappear into the darkness, slipped into the kiosk and recorded *El bulín de la calle Ayacucho (Our little Room on Ayacucho)*, trying to imitate the version Gardel sang with José Ricardo accompanying him on guitar.

When he finished, the technician in the booth asked him to sing it again, because the acetate looked scratched. Estéfano repeated the tango, nervously, at a quicker pace. He feared his mother would have finished the ride by then and might be looking for him.

What's your name, lad? the technician asked.

Estéfano. But I'm thinking of finding one that sounds more artistic.

With that voice you needn't bother. You've got sunlight in your throat.

The boy hid the record under his shirt. It was the second version, which had come out worse, but he was lucky enough to get back before his mother reappeared from her third trip round on the ghost train.

For a while he went around looking for a gramophone where he could hear his recording in secret, but he didn't know anyone who had one, especially for 45 rpm discs like the one they'd sold him at the kiosk. The acetate was affected by heat, humidity and the dust that accumulated between the issues of *20th Century Songbirds*. Estéfano thought his recorded voice must have disappeared forever, but one Saturday night, while he was in the kitchen with his mother listening to the popular program *Stairway to Fame* on the radio, one of the announcers said that the revelation of the moment was an anonymous singer who had recorded an a cappella version of *Our little room on Ayacucho* in some unknown studio. Thanks to the miracle of magnetic tapes, he said, the voice was now backed up by a violin and bandoneón accompaniment. Estéfano immediately recognized the first recording, which the technician had pretended to discard, and he went pale. Separated from his own voice, he found himself still connected to it by a thread of the kind of admiration it was only possible to feel towards something we don't possess. It wasn't a voice he would have wanted or sought but something that had alighted in his throat. Since it was alien to his body, it could be removed when he least expected it. Who knew how many times it had been around in the past and how many other voices fit within it. To Estéfano it mattered only that it resembled one voice: Carlos Gardel's. So he was flattered by his mother's comment as they listened to *Stairway to Fame*:

Hey, isn't that strange? They're saying it's an unknown singer but it's not. If he was accompanied by José Ricardo's guitar, you'd swear it was Gardel.

At that spur to his pride, the voice slipped out:

That little room on Ayacucho / now feels uninviting and shoddy . . .

Estéfano stopped himself before going on to the next line, but it was too late. His mother said:

You sound just like him.

It's not me, Estéfano defended himself.

I know it's not you. How are you going to be on the

radio if you're here? But you could be there if you wanted. Why don't you sing in the clubs? All this sewing's ruining my eyes.

Estéfano went to one or two trattorias in Villa Urquiza, but he didn't even get an audition. He wasn't accompanied by a guitarist, like most singers, and the owners feared his appearance would scare off the clientele. Since he didn't dare go home without having earned a bit of money, he made use of his faultless memory to take bets on the pools. He was hired by a funeral director who ran a gambling den, connected to the race tracks and the lotteries, in offices adjacent to the chapels of rest. From there Estéfano answered telephone queries about the prices of burials at the same time as he took the wagers. He remembered how much money a certain client had bet on the three final numbers of the lottery grand prize and how much someone else had placed on the last figure, as well as knowing where to find each gambler at different times of day. When the police raided the funeral parlor after an anonymous tip-off, they couldn't find the slightest evidence against Estéfano because all the details of every stake were in his head.

He spent several years at these mnemotechnical activities and would perhaps have kept at it all his life if the owner of the funeral parlor hadn't rewarded him by giving in to his pleas that he enter him in the singing competition at the Sunderland Club. The prizes were decided by popular vote: each ticket holder got one vote, which turned the atmosphere in the hall into that of an electoral campaign. Estéfano had little chance and he knew it. The only thing that mattered to him, however, was that the voice, hidden for so many years, should finally flow out into the light of the world.

The celebrated baritone Antonio Rossi had a string of ten Saturday night triumphs at the Sunderland, and he'd announced he would be participating again. His repertoire was predictable: he only sang tangos that were currently fashionable and easy to dance to. Estéfano, on the other hand, had decided to compete with a tango from 1920, avoiding lyrics with double entendres to keep from offending the ladies.

The funeral parlor was frequently closed due to a lack of the deceased. Estéfano took advantage of those times to practice *Mano a mano (Now We're Even)*, a tango by Celedonio Flores which ended on a note of unexpected generosity. After wavering between others by Pascual Contursi and Ángel Villoldo, he'd decided on his mother's favorite. For hours among the empty coffins he imitated Gardel's poses, with the rolled-up scarf around his neck. He learned that he could appear more elegant if he did without his stick and held the microphone while sitting on a stool.

The night before the contest, in the funeral parlor waiting room, he found an old supplement from the newspaper *La Nación* devoted to the author of a single novel who had died very young of tuberculosis. The novelist's real name, José María Miró, meant nothing to him. His pseudonym, however, had such assonance with the phonemes of Carlos Gardel, that he decided to appropriate it. Calling himself Julián Martel, like the unfortunate writer the supplement was about, might cause confusion; choosing Carlos Martel

26

would practically be plagiarism. So, he opted to be Julio Martel. When he entered the competition he'd left off his ridiculous surname, calling himself simply Estéfano. Now he asked to be introduced under his new identity.

At seven in the evening one Saturday in November, the master of ceremonies introduced the young tenor for the first time. He'd been preceded by seven singers with mediocre voices. The hall's attention was suspended in anticipation of Antonio Rossi, who was going to repeat, by popular request, *En esta tarde gris (On This Grey Evening)*, by Mores and Contursi. The dance floor was a basketball court they'd taken the hoops out of, which would be used the next day for a children's soccer tournament. It had a platform at the back with music stands for the two accompanying violinists. The singers usually sang too close to the microphone and their interpretations were interrupted by screeches of discouraging static. Some impatient fans preferred to chat or wait out on the sidewalk. Most of them were only interested in Rossi's entry, the invariable result of the competition, and the dance that would follow, with recorded music by the big orchestras.

Before going on stage, Estéfano, who was now definitively Julio Martel, knew he was going to lose. Standing in the corridor, looking at his shiny suit, the oversized collar of his shirt and the clumsy bow tie in a mirror, he grew disheartened. His brilliantined hairstyle, which had gleamed at four o'clock in the afternoon, had dissolved into a fog of dandruff by seven. In the hall he was greeted by the timid clapping of Señora Olivia and three neighbors. As he walked towards the stool, he thought he could discern a murmur of pity. When the violins struck up *Mano a mano*, he took courage by imagining himself on the prow of a ship, irresistible like Gardel.

Perhaps his gestures were a parody of those seen in the immortal singer's films. But the voice was unique. It took off by itself, unfurling more emotions than fit into an entire lifetime and, of course, far more than Celedonio Flores' tango modestly hinted at. *Mano a mano* told the story of a woman who left the man she loved for a life of riches and pleasure. Martel turned it into a mystic lament on mortal flesh and the solitude of the soul without God.

The violins were out of tune and out of time, but they were masked by the density of the singing that advanced like a fury, transforming everything it touched into gold. Estéfano's diction was defective: he left off the final s's of the words and simplified the sound of the x's in exuberance and examine. Gardel, in the version of *Mano a mano* with José Ricardo on guitar, says *carta* instead of *canta* and *conesejo* instead of *consejo*. Martel caressed the syllables as if they were glass and poured them out intact over an enchanted audience, silent since the first verse.

They gave him a standing ovation. Some enthusiastic women, breaking the rules of the competition, shouted for an encore. Martel left the stage in a state of confusion and had to lean on his stick. From a bench in the corridor, he listened to another singer imitating the neighing of Alberto Castillo. Then he shuddered at the round of applause that greeted Rossi as he took the stage. The first lines of *En esta tarde gris*, which his rival let fall with his colorless voice, convinced him that something worse than defeat would happen that night. He would be forgotten. The vote confirmed, as usual, Rossi's overwhelming supremacy.

Mario Virgili was fifteen years old then and his parents had taken him to the Sunderland Club to instill in him a love for the tango. Virgili supposed that Rossi, Gardel, Troilo's orchestra and that of Julio De Caro embodied all that the genre had to offer. In 1976, the atrocious dictatorship forced him into exile, where he remained for a little over eight years. One night, in the city of Caracas, while he was in a bookstore on the Sabana Grande Boulevard, he heard in the distance the opening bars of *Mano a mano* and felt an invincible nostalgia. The melody buzzed around Virgili's memory for hours in an infinite present that didn't want to give way. He'd heard it hundreds of times, sung by Gardel, by Charlo, by Alberto Arenas, by Goyeneche. Nevertheless, the voice that settled in his head was that of Martel. For Virgili, that fleeting moment one November Saturday in the Sunderland had been transfigured into a breath of eternity.

People disappeared by the thousand during those years, and the singer also faded into the routine of the funeral parlor, where he worked seventy hours a week. The pools had been legalized, so the owner set up baccarat and poker tables in the back, on top of the empty coffins. Martel had the gift of knowing which cards would turn up in each hand, and signaled to the dealers by a system of gestures how they should play. Many unemployed workers and technicians turned up, and at each table there was so much tension, such desire to domesticate luck, that Martel felt pangs of conscience for accentuating the ruin of those desperate men.

In the spring of 1981, a colonel ordered a raid on the gambling den. The owner of the funeral parlor was tried but acquitted due to procedural errors. Martel, however, spent six months in the notorious Villa Devoto prison. That misfortune left him even thinner and smaller. His cheekbones stuck out, his eyes looked darker and bulged from his gaunt face, but the voice remained intact, immune to illness and failure.

Virgili, who had been an encyclopedia salesman in Venezuela, went into business with two friends when he returned from exile and set up a bookstore on Corrientes Street, where there were already twenty or thirty others and lots of shoppers. It was an instant success. People stayed to chat until the early hours between the tables of special offers, and he soon felt obliged to add a café, which encouraged spontaneous guitarists and poets.

The months flew by in a blur, not knowing where they were headed, as if the past were innocent of the future. One night in 1985, in the bookstore, someone mentioned a marvelous tenor who was singing in a little place over in Boedo for whatever they felt like paying him. It was difficult to understand the lyrics of his tangos, which reproduced an ancient and now meaningless language. The tenor had a refined way of pronouncing them, but the words wouldn't let themselves be caught: *You donked the little strumple / up against a bamp in the creamery*. They were all like that, or almost all. Sometimes, among the six or seven tangos he sang a night, one or two would come up that the oldest of his listeners could identify, though not without effort, like *Mucked up with Yeast* or *I got Gut Rot from your Manger*, of which there are no records or sheet music.

In the first appearances, when a flutist accompanied the tenor, the songs revealed mischief, sexual happiness, perpetual youth. Later the flutist was replaced by an impassive, serious bandoneón player, who darkened the repertoire. Fed up with songs they couldn't decipher, the more conventional clients stopped coming. Instead, more imaginative listeners began to frequent the place, amazed by a voice that, rather than repeating images and stories, slid from one emotion to another, with the clarity of a sonata. Like the music, the voice had no need of meaning. It expressed itself alone.

Virgili had a hunch this was the same person who'd sung *Mano a mano* in the Sunderland twenty-two years earlier. The following Saturday he went to the place in Boedo. As he watched the slight and spidery Martel move towards the platform beside the counter, and listened to him sing, he realized that this voice eluded any description because it was itself the tale of the past and future of Buenos Aires. Suspended by a tenuous thread of Cs and Fs, the voice hinted at the massacre of the Unitarians, Manuelita Rosas' passion for her father, the Revolution of the Park, the overcrowding and despair of immigrants, the slaughter of the Tragic Week in 1919, the bombing of the Plaza de

Mayo before the fall of Perón, Pedro Henríquez Ureña chasing death down the platforms of Constitución Station, the dictator Onganía censoring Bach's Magnificat and the enchantment of the artists Noé, Deira and De la Vega in the Di Tella Institute, the failures of a city that had every possible advantage yet had nothing. Martel let all this pour out like thousand-year-old water.

Come and sing in El Rufián Melancólico bookstore, Virgili proposed to him when the show finished. I can pay you and your bandoneonist a fixed salary.

Fixed salary, imagine that. Didn't know there was such a thing anymore.

His speaking voice bore absolutely no relation to the voice he sang with: it was reticent and uneducated. The man it came from seemed different from the one who sang. He wore a ridiculous signet ring glittering with gemstones on the little finger of his left hand. The veins of both hands were swollen and had needle marks.

There is, said Virgili. On Corrientes Street more people would hear you. Which is what you deserve, sir.

He didn't dare drop the formalities. Martel, on the other hand, answered while looking the other way.

What comes here ain't so bad, man. Let me hear the deal and I'll think it over.

He started to sing at El Rufián the following Friday. Six months later they took him to the Club del Vino, where he shared the bill with Horacio Salgán, Ubaldo de Lío and the bandoneón player Néstor Marconi. Although his tangos were more and more abstruse and remote, the voice rose with such purity that people recognized in it feelings they'd lost or forgotten, and burst into tears or laughter without the slightest embarrassment. The night Jean Franco went to El Club del Vino they gave him a ten-minute standing ovation. He would have gone on like that for who knows how long if an intestinal hemorrhage hadn't put him back in the hospital.

Martel's hemophilia, caused by the lack of factor 8, was accompanied by a retinue of illnesses. He frequently succumbed to malignant fevers or pneumonia. He was often covered in scabs that he hid with makeup. None of his admirers knew that he arrived to sing in a wheelchair or that he couldn't have walked more than three steps across the stage. Near the curtain there was always a stool screwed to the floor, which he'd lean on as he sang after bowing his head slightly. It had been quite some time since he'd been able to imitate Gardel's gestures and, although nothing would have pleased him more, his style had gained in frugality and a certain bodily invisibility. So the voice glittered on its own, as if nothing else existed in the world, not even the accompanying bandoneón in the background.

The intestinal bleeding put him out of circulation for a few years. Months before I arrived in Buenos Aires he had started singing again. He didn't sing when asked anymore but only when he felt like it. Instead of returning to El Rufián or El Club del Vino, where they still longed to hear him, he would appear out of the blue in the dance halls in the neighborhoods of San Telmo or Villa Urquiza, or he offered open air concerts in some part of the city, for whoever wanted to hear him. To his repertoire of bygone tangos he began adding those composed by Gardel and Le Pera, and some of Cadícamo's classics.

One night he sang from the balcony of one of the hotels for furtive lovers on the Azcuénaga Street, behind Recoleta Cemetery. Many couples interrupted the clamor of their passion and listened to the powerful voice infiltrating through the windows and bathing their bodies forever in a tango they'd never heard before, in a language they didn't understand, but which they recognized as if it came from a previous life. One of the witnesses told Virgili that a sheet of aurora borealis shone in an arc over the crosses and arch-angels of the cemetery, and after the song everyone there felt a guiltless peace.

He showed up in unusual places that held no special interest to anyone, or perhaps they were points on a map of some other Buenos Aires. After a recital in Retiro Station, he announced that he would one day be going down into the canal through which flowed the Maldonado stream, under Juan B. Justo Avenue, which crosses the city from east to west, to sing a tango there that no one now remembered, whose rhythm was an indiscernible blend of *habaneras*, *milongas* and *rancheras*.

However, he sang in another tunnel first: the one that opens like a delta beneath the obelisk at the Plaza de la República, at the intersection of 9 de Julio Avenue and Corrientes Street. The place is inappropriate for his voice, because sounds carry for eighteen or twenty feet and then suddenly die out. At one of the entrances is a string of chairs with footrests for the few passersby who might want their shoes shined, and tiny stools for those who serve them. There are lots of posters of soccer teams and *Playboy* bunnies around them. Two of the branches lead to kiosks and shops selling army surplus, second-hand magazines and papers, shoelaces and insoles, homemade perfumes, stamps, handbags and wallets, industrial reproductions of Picasso's *Guernica* and *Paloma*, umbrellas and socks.

Martel didn't sing in those populous labyrinthine detours but in one of the dead-end hollows where some homeless families had set up camp. Any voice there drops like lead as soon as it leaves the throat: the density of the air forces it down. But Martel was heard in all the tributaries of the tunnels because his voice swerved around the obstacles like a thread of water. It was the only time he sang *Caminito (Little Path)*, by Filiberto and Coria Peñaloza, a tango inferior to the demands of his repertoire. Virgili thought he'd done it because everyone around there could follow the words without getting lost, and because he didn't want to add another enigma to an underground labyrinth where there were already so many.

No one knew why Martel performed in such inhospitable places, without charging a cent. At the end of the spring of 2001 there were lots of clubs, theaters, bars and *milongas* in Buenos Aires that would have welcomed him with open arms. Perhaps he was ashamed of exposing a body mercilessly abused by illness day after day. He spent two weeks in hospital with fibrosis of the liver. Sometimes he got nosebleeds. His arthrosis was relentless. Still, when no one expected it, he showed up at these absurd locations and sang for himself.

Those recitals must have had a meaning that only he knew, and I said so to Virgili. I proposed to find out if the places Martel went to were linked by some order or plan. Any logical device or the repetition of a detail could reveal the complete sequence and allow me to get to his next appearance ahead of him. I was convinced the outings had to do with a Buenos Aires we didn't see and during an entire morning I amused myself composing anagrams from the name of the city, without getting anywhere. The ones I did come up with were stupid: Serious bean / Bruise a nose / Easier on bus / I sane, U sober.

One afternoon, about two, Martel went all the way into the Waterworks Palace, where the ironwork footbridges, the valves, tanks, pipes and columns, which one hundred years before had distributed seventy-two thousand tons of drinking water to the inhabitants of Buenos Aires, were still preserved intact. I heard that he'd sung another obscure tango there and left in a wheelchair. So, it wasn't important to him to repeat the patterns of history, because history doesn't move, doesn't speak, everything in it has already been said. He wanted, rather, to recover a past city that only he knew and transfigure it into the present of a city he'd take with him when he died.

TWO

October 2001

As the days went by, I began to figure out that Buenos Aires, designed by its two successive founders as a perfect checkerboard, had turned into a labyrinth that occurred not just in space, as they all did, but also in time. I frequently attempted to go somewhere and found I couldn't, because hundreds of people were waving signs protesting against unemployment and salary cuts. One afternoon I wanted to cross Diagonal Norte Avenue to get to Florida Street, and a fierce wall of indignant demonstrators, beating a drum, obliged me to make a detour. Two of the women raised their hands as if greeting me and I replied in kind. I must have done something I shouldn't have because they spat at me, hurling insults I'd never heard and didn't then know the meaning of: 'You a rat, informer, faggot? Did you get a good pay-off? What'd they paid you?' A woman tried to hit me, and they held her back. Two hours later, when I was going back along the street where the Cathedral is, I ran into them again and feared the worst. But by then they seemed tired and ignored me.

What happened with people also happened with places:

they constantly changed their mood, seriousness, language. One of Buenos Aires inhabitants' regular expressions is: 'I can't find myself here,' which is the equivalent of saying 'I'm not myself here.' A few days after arriving I visited the house at 994 Maipú Street where Borges had lived for more than forty years, and I had the sensation that I'd seen it somewhere else or, which was worse, that it was a scene destined to disappear as soon as I turned my back. I took some photographs and, when I got them developed, I noticed that the entrance hall had been transformed in a subtle way and the floor tiles were arranged in a different pattern.

Something worse happened to me with Julio Martel. No matter how hard I tried, I couldn't attend any of his performances, which were extravagant and sporadic. Someone told me where he lived and I spent hours waiting outside the door to his house until I saw him come out. He was short, with thick, black hair, stiffened with hairspray and lacquer. He hopped along like a lobster, perhaps leaning on a cane. I tried to follow him in a taxi and lost him near the Plaza del los Dos Congresos, at a corner cut off by a teachers' demonstration. I had the feeling that in the Buenos Aires of those months the threads of reality moved out of step with the people and were weaving a labyrinth in which no one could find anything, or anyone.

El Tucumano told me that some companies organized guided hour or two-hour-long tours for Europeans who disembarked at Ezeiza airport on their way to the glaciers of

Patagonia, Iguazú Falls or the inlets of Puerto Madryn, where the whales went mad as they thunderously gave birth. The buses often got lost among the ruins of the Camino Negro or in the quagmires of La Boca and wouldn't reappear for days, and even then the passengers would have no memory of whatever it was that had held them up.

They muddle them up with all kinds of gimmicks, El Tucumano told me. One of the excursions went to all the big soccer stadiums simulating a day of classic matches. They get a hundred tourists together and go from the River Plate stadium to Boca's, and from there to Vélez' ground in Liniers. By the gates of each they have people selling chorizos, t-shirts, pennants, while the stadium loudspeakers reproduce the roar of a non-existent crowd, which the visitors imagine to be there. They've even written articles about this fakery, El Tucumano said, and I wondered who the authors might have been: Albert Camus, Bruce Chatwin, Naipaul, Madonna? They were each shown a Buenos Aires that doesn't exist, or maybe they could only see the one they'd already imagined before their arrival. There are also tours of the meat processing plants, El Tucumano went on, and another one for twenty pesos of the famous cafés. At around seven in the evening they take the tourists for a walk down the Avenida de Mayo, through San Telmo and Barracas, to see the cafés. In the Café Tortoni they set up a show for them with dice players who flourish their shakers and threaten each other with daggers. They listen to tango singers in El Querandí, and in

El Progreso on Montes de Oca Avenue they chat with novelists working away on their laptops. It's all a front, all a set-up, as you can imagine.

What I didn't know then was that there was also a municipal excursion devoted to Borges' Buenos Aires, until I saw the tourists pull up at the boarding house on Garay Street, one November day at noon, in a bus with the lurid McDonald's monogram on each side. Almost all of them were from Iceland or Denmark and they were on their way to the southern lakes, where the landscapes might surprise them less than the endless solitude. They spoke in a guttural English, which permitted intermittent conversations, as if the distance might leave the words hanging in mid-air. I understood they'd paid thirty dollars for a walk that began at nine in the morning and ended just before one. The pamphlet they'd been given to help find their way was a sheet of newsprint folded in four with lots of ads for masseurs who did home visits, rest clinics and euphoria-producing pills freely for sale. In the midst of this typographical jungle, one could just make out the points of the itinerary, explained in a peculiar English twisted by Spanish syntax.

The first stop on the route was Borges' birthplace, the house at 840 Tucumán Street, at a time when the Saturday morning traffic is tangled and short-tempered. There, the tour guide – a short young woman with her hair in a bun and the gestures of a primary school teacher – read an extract from the 'Autobiographical Essay' that described the place at breakneck speed: a *flat roof; a long, arched entranceway called a* zaguán; *a cistern, where we got our water; and two patios*.

God knows how the Scandinavians imagined the cistern, or rather the well, with a pulley at the top and a water bucket hanging from it. In any case, none of that was still standing. On the site of the original house stood a building with three names: *Solar Natal, Café Literario* and *Fundación Internacional Jorge Luis Borges*. The façade was glass, and gave a view of wrought-iron tables and chairs, with unbleached fabric cushions tied onto the seats. At the back, in the open-air patio, you could make out more tables with parasols and several colored balloons, perhaps left over from a children's party. Across the façade, like a blindfold, stretched a painted strip of dusty pink. The building on the right, which belonged to the YWCA, at number 848, also claimed the right to be considered the site of the birthplace. It sported a shiny bronze plaque, which protested against changes to the numbering of the street and maintained that, since 1899, the buildings had shifted from their original locations and the whole street was slipping down the slope of the river bank, even though the river itself was at least three-quarters of a mile away.

The tour's itinerary was thrifty. It cut out the poor sections of Palermo and Pompeya, where Borges had walked till daybreak when those places ended suddenly in open countryside, in a vast empty horizon after alleyways, cigar shops and vegetable gardens. It omitted, most of all, the block from the poem 'The Mythical Founding of Buenos Aires,' where the writer had lived from the age of two until he was fourteen, before his family moved to Geneva, and where he had the intuition, later confirmed by

43

the idealist philosopher Francis Herbert Bradley, that time is an incessant agony of the present disintegrating into the past.

The woman with the bun had informed the passengers that the spot where Buenos Aires had been founded was in the Plaza de Mayo, because it was there that Juan de Garay, from Vizcaya, planted a tree of justice on June 11th 1580, and cleared the land with his sword, chopping away the pastures and reeds as a sign of his taking possession of the city and the port. Forty-four years earlier Pedro de Mendoza, from Granada, had done the same thing in Parque Lezama, another square half a league to the south, but then the city had been evacuated and burnt, while Mendoza was dying of syphilis on his ship.

Since Buenos Aires was born, a strange series of calamities tormented her founders. Mendoza's crews mutinied twice; one of his ships strayed off course and ended up in the Caribbean; his soldiers were starving to death and resorted to cannibalism; and almost all the forts he left along his course were destroyed by sudden fires. Garay also faced rebellions in his garrisons on land, but the worst disturbance happened in his head. In 1581 he set off in search of the illusory City of the Caesars, which he imagined in dreams as an island of giants guarded by dragons and griffins, in its center a temple made of gold and garnet that shone in the darkness. He traveled more than a hundred leagues down the pot-bellied coast of Samborombón and the South Atlantic without finding a trace of what he'd imagined. On his return, he could no longer find his way through reality and, to recover his reason, he had to find it in his dreams. In March of 1583, while traveling in a brigantine toward Carcarañá, he stopped after dark in a network of streams and canals with no apparent exit. He decided to camp on dry land and await the morning with his crew of fifty Spaniards. He did not live to see it. A party of Querandí scouts attacked before dawn and tore his dream to shreds with their spears.

From the birthplace, the visitors were taken to the house on Maipú Street, where Borges lived in a monastic room, separated from his mother's bedroom by a wooden partition wall. It was such a narrow cell that it barely held a bed, a nightstand and a desk. Examining this now faded privacy was not part of the excursion. The tourists were allowed only a brief stop in front of the house, and a more generous visit to La Ciudad bookstore, which was across the street, where Borges went in the mornings to dictate poems his blindness wouldn't allow him to write down.

In spite of the rush, up till then the walk had been calm, upset only by the rage of the drivers obliged to stop behind the bus, and the hell of honking horns, which more than once had convinced Borges that he should move to a silent suburb. Until that point in the morning, when it was not much past ten, nothing had yet disconcerted the passengers. They recognized the spots on the itinerary because they figured, although in less detail, in the Scandinavian guidebooks. The first breach of the routine struck when, at the request of the municipal tour guide, they ventured on foot down Florida Street, from the intersection with Paraguay Street, following the route Borges took almost daily on his way to the National Library. Everything was different from what the thirty-year-old stories suggested, and even from what the detailed guidebooks from Copenhagen said. The street – which at the end of the nineteenth century had been an elegant promenade and, later, during the 1960s, the vanguard space, the place for madness, for challenges to reality and order – on that Saturday morning was a reproduction of one of those clamorous, open-air Central American markets. Hundreds of peddlers had stretched out blankets and cloths to the middle of the road where they displayed objects as useless as they were eye-catching: gigantic pencils and combs, stiff, straight belts, china teapots with the spout raised up towards the handle, charcoal-sketched portraits that looked completely different from the model.

Grete Amundsen, one of the Danish tourists, stopped to buy a *maté* gourd made of cactus wood, which would let the boiling water drain out as soon as it was poured into it. While she examined the object and admired its design, which reminded her of something she'd read about the mammary glands of whales, Grete was left at the center of a circle that suddenly formed on the street around a couple of tango dancers. Since she was the tallest person on the tour – when I saw her, I estimated she was over six feet tall – she helplessly watched what was happening as if she were in a box at the theater. She felt as though she'd accidentally entered a mistaken dream. She saw her companions disappearing down the street. She called to them with all the force in her lungs, but there was no sound that could have risen above the din of that morning fair. She saw three violinists moving forward into the clearing where she was a prisoner, and heard them play a melody she didn't recognize. The tango dancers executed a baroque choreography, from which Grete tried to escape while running from one side to the other, finding no cracks in the increasingly compact crowd. Finally someone let her through, but only to leave her enclosed in a second human wall. She elbowed and kicked her way through, uttering curses of which only the word *fuck* could be understood. She could no longer see any trace of her friends. Nor did she recognize the place where she was. In the jumble she'd been relieved of her purse but she didn't have any courage left to go back and look for it. The merchants she saw when she came out of the tumult were the same; the street, however, was suddenly different. In an identical succession to that of minutes before, she saw the cloths piled with combs and belts, teapots and pendants, as well as the guy selling the *maté* gourds, for whom time seemed not to have moved. 'Florida?' she asked, and the man, lifting his chin to point out the sign above her head, which clearly read Lavalle. 'Is not Florida?' she said disconsolately. 'Lavalle,' the vendor informed her. 'This is called Lavalle.' Grete felt the world was disappearing. It was her second morning in the city, up till then she had allowed herself to be taken from place to place by obliging guides, and she didn't remember the name of the hotel. Panamericano, Interamericano, Sudamericano? They all sounded the same. She still held, crumpled in her hand, the pamphlet with the itinerary of the excursion. She was relieved to cling to those words of which she under-

47

stood only one, Florida. She followed, on the rough map, the course her friends would have taken: *Florida, Perú until México. The Writer's House. Ex National Library.* Maybe the bus with the McDonald's ads would be waiting for them there, at that last stop. She saw in the distance a slow procession of taxis. The previous afternoon she'd learned that in Buenos Aires there were more than thirty thousand, and almost all their drivers tried to show, at the first opportunity, that the job was beneath them. The one who brought her from the airport to the hotel gave her a lecture on superconductivity, in passable English; another, in the evening, criticized the idea of sin in *Fear and Trembling*, by Kierkegaard, or at least that's what Grete deduced from the title of the book and displeasure of the driver. The guide explained that, although educated, some taxi drivers were dangerous. They drove tourists to some out-of-the-way spot, picked up an accomplice and fleeced them. How to tell them from legitimate ones? No one knew. The safest thing was to take a car that someone was getting out of, but it all came down to luck. The city was full of empty taxis.

Knowing she had no money, Grete signaled to a young driver with tangled hair. Which way do you want to go? Through the Bajo or down 9 de Julio? These were the usual questions, to which she'd already learned the answer: 'Whichever. Ex National Library.' Her companions from the excursion couldn't take more than an hour. The itinerary was strict. One of them would lend her a few pesos.

As they went, the avenues became wider and wider, and the air, although occasionally disturbed by plastic bags that rose in sudden flight, was clearer. The taxi's radio emitted constant orders that alluded to an infinite city, incomprehensible to Grete: 'Federico wait at 3873 Rómulo Naón, second charlie, ten to fifteen minutes. Kika at the front door of the school, Colegio del Pilar, identify by Kika, seven to ten minutes. Let's see, who's near Práctico Poliza Street in Barracas, avoid Congreso, alpha four, there's a demonstration of doctors there and they've closed off Rivadavia, Entre Ríos, Combate de los Pozos.' And so on. They passed a solitary red tower, in the center of a plaza, beside a long wall that protected innumerable steel containers. Further on was a park, a heavy, dark building that resembled the Reichstag in Berlin, and then a gigantic sculpture of a metal flower. In the distance, on the left, a solid tower, supported by four Herculean columns, seemed to be the destination point.

There it is. The Library, announced the taxi driver.

He drove down Agüero Street, stopped beside a marble stairway and showed her the ramp to go up to get to the tower. See the sign over the entrance, he said, isn't this where you wanted to go?

Could you please wait just one minute? Grete asked.

At the top of the ramp there was a terrace interrupted by a truncated pyramid, with an extractor fan on top. The fact that the McDonald's bus had not arrived intensified her sense of emptiness and desertion. She perceived only what was not there and, therefore, didn't even perceive herself. From one of the terrace parapets she looked over the gardens opposite and the statues that cut into the horizon. It was the Library, the sign was unequivocal. Nevertheless, she was overwhelmed by a feeling of loss. At some moment during the morning, perhaps when she went from Florida Street to Lavalle Street without knowing how, all the points of the city had got tangled up. Even the maps she'd seen the previous evening were confused, because the west was invariably in the north, and the center was tipped out over the eastern edge.

The taxi driver came over without her noticing. A slight breeze stirred up his hair, now towering, electrified.

Look over there, to the left, he pointed.

Grete followed the direction of his hand.

That's the statue of Pope John Paul II, and the other one, above the avenue, is Evita Perón. There's also a map of the neighborhood, see? That's Recoleta, with the cemetery to one side.

She understood the names, Evita, *the Pope*? However, the figures were unconnected to the place. They both had their backs to the building and all it stood for. Could that really be the Library? She was starting to get used to words being in one place and what they meant being somewhere else entirely.

She tried to explain, in hand signals, her disorientation and dispossession. The language was insufficient to put forward something so simple, and the hand movements, instead of clarifying things, tended to modify them. The voice of an animal would have made more sense: the emission of unmodulated sounds indicating desperation, loss. Ex Library, Grete attempted. Ex, Ex.

But this is the Library, the driver said. Don't you see we're here?

Two hours later, in front of the entrance to the boarding house on Garay Street, while she told the story to her traveling companions and I summed it up for the manager and El Tucumano, Grete still hadn't determined when they'd begun to understand each other. It was like a sudden pentecost, she said: the gift of languages descended and lit them from within. Maybe she'd pointed out to the taxi driver some Rosetta stone on the map, maybe he knew that the word Borges would decipher codes and guessed that the Library in question was the extinct, the exanime, the ex, a city without books that languished in the far south of Buenos Aires. Ah, it's the other one, the young man had said to her. I've taken more than a few musicians to that place: I've taken violins, clarinets, guitars, saxophones, bassoons, people who are exorcising the ghost of Borges because, as you'll know, he was blind musically as well. He couldn't tell Mozart from Haydn and he hated the tango. No he didn't, I said, correcting Grete when she repeated this detail. He felt that the Genoese immigrants had corrupted it. Borges didn't even appreciate Gardel, the taxi driver had told her. Once he went to the cinema to see Josef von Sternberg's *Underworld*, back when they used to have live acts in between one film and the next. Gardel was going to sing during the intermission and Borges got irritated, stood up and left. That's true: he wasn't interested in Gardel, I told Grete. He would have preferred one of those improvisers who sang in the local bars in the outskirts at the beginning of the twentieth century, but when Borges returned from his long trip to Europe, in 1921, there were no longer any worth listening to.

Grete's shipwrecks of that morning were now a cause for celebration. She'd seen another Buenos Aires from the taxi, she said: a red brick wall beyond which rose marble flowers, Masonic compasses, angels with trumpets; there you have the labyrinth of the dead – the young man with the tangled hair had told her – they've buried all of Argentina's past beneath that sea of crosses, and, nevertheless, at the entrance to that cemetery – Grete told us – there were two colossal trees, two rubber trees rising out of some ageless swamp, that defied time and survived destruction and misfortune, especially because the roots braided together and the tops reached for the light of the sky. Scandinavian skies were never so crystal clear. Grete was still contemplating it when the taxi turned off down some tedious streets and came out in a triangular plaza on which stood three or four palaces copied from those on Avenue Foch, please stop here for a moment, Grete had begged, while she observed the luxurious windows, the empty balconies and clear sky above. That was when she remembered a novel by George Orwell, *Coming Up For Air*, that she'd read in adolescence, in which a character called George Bowling describes himself like this: 'I'm fat, but I'm thin inside. Has it ever struck you that there's a thin man inside every fat man, just as they say there's a statue inside every block of stone?' That was Buenos Aires, Grete said to herself at that moment and repeated to us later: a delta of cities embraced by one single city, a myriad of tiny, thin cities within this obese unique majesty that allows Madrid-style avenues and Catalan cafés next to Neapolitan aviaries and Doric bandstands and Rive Droite mansions, beyond all of which, however – the taxi driver had insisted – were the livestock market, with the lowing of the cattle before sacrifice and the smell of dung, the evening dew, the open plain, and also a melancholy that comes from nowhere except here, from the end of the earth feeling you get when you look at maps and see how alone Buenos Aires is, how very out of the way.

When we turned onto 9 de Julio Avenue and saw the obelisk in the center, I felt sad thinking we'd be leaving in two days' time, Grete said. If I could be born again, I would choose Buenos Aires and I wouldn't move from this place even if they stole my purse again with a hundred pesos and my Helsingør driver's license in it, because I can live without those but not without the light of the sky I saw this morning.

She'd arrived at Borges' National Library, on México Street, almost at the same time as her tired companions. There too they had to settle for the façade, inspired by the Milanese Renaissance. When the guide had the group gathered on the sidewalk in front of the building, among broken flagstones and piles of dog shit, she informed them that, completed in 1901, it was originally destined for the lottery draws and that's why there were so many winged nymphs with unseeing eyes, which represented chance, and large bronze drums. The spiderweb of shelves rose through circular labyrinths that emerged, if you knew your way, into a corridor of low ceilings, adjacent to a cupola open over the abyss of books. The reading room had been stripped of its tables and lamps more than a decade earlier, and the premises were now used for symphony orchestra rehearsals. 'National Music Center,' read the sign at the entrance, beside the defiant doors. On the right-hand wall, there was a slogan written in black aerosol paint: 'Democracy lasts as long as obedience.' An anarchist wrote that, said the guide disparagingly. See how they signed it with an A inside a circle.

That was the penultimate stop before they arrived at the boarding house where I lived. The bus drove them through potholed streets to a café, at the corner of Chile and Tacuarí, where – according to the guide – Borges had written desperate love letters to the woman who turned down his marriage proposals over and over again and who he tried in vain to seduce by dedicating 'The Aleph' to her, while waiting to see her come out of the building to approach her if only with a look. *I miss you unceasingly*, he told her. His writing, 'my dwarf's handwriting,' ran in lines that sloped further and further downwards, in a sign of sadness or devotion, *Estela, Estela Canto, when you read this I shall be finishing the story I promised you*. Borges could only express his love in an exalted, sighing English, he was afraid of tarnishing with his sentiments the language of the tale he was writing.

I've always thought the character of Beatriz Viterbo, the woman who dies at the beginning of 'The Aleph,' was a direct descendent of Estela Canto's, I told the Scandinavians when they were gathered in the front hall of the boarding house.

During the months he spent writing the story, Borges was passionately reading Dante. He'd purchased the three small volumes of Melville Anderson's translation in the Oxford bilingual edition, and at some moment must have felt that Estela could guide him to Paradise just as Beatriz, Beatrice, had allowed him to see the aleph. They were both in the past by the time he finished the tale; both had been cruel, haughty, negligent, scornful, and to both, the imaginary and the real, he owed 'the best and perhaps the worst hours of my life,' as he'd written in the last of his letters to Estela.

I don't know how much of this could have interested the tourists, who were anxious to see – impossible though it was – the aleph.

Before the guided tour of the boarding house began, El Tucumano took me by the arm and dragged me into the closet where Enriqueta kept the keys and the cleaning supplies.

If the Alé isn't a person, then what's with it? he asked me with a touch of impatience.

'The Aleph,' I said, is a short story by Borges. And also, according to the story, it's a point in space that contains all points, the story of the universe in a single place and a single instant.

How weird. A point.

Borges described it as a small iridescent sphere of blinding light. It's down in a cellar, when you get to the nineteenth step.

And these characters have come to see it?

That's what they want, but the aleph doesn't exist.

If they wanna see it, we've gotta show it to 'em.

Enriqueta was calling me and I had to go. In Borges' story the façade of Beatriz Viterbo's house is not mentioned, but the tour guide had already decided it was like the one we were looking at, of stone and granite, with a tall wrought-iron door and a balcony on the right, plus two more balconies on the upper floor, one spacious and curved, which belonged to my room, and another paltry one, almost the size of a window, which was undoubtedly the scandalous neighbors'. The small cluttered drawing room mentioned in the story was just past the threshold of the entrance hall and then, at one end of what had been the dining room and was now the reception area, was the way to the cellar, to which one descended down nineteen steep steps.

When the house was converted into rooms to let, the administrator had ordered that the trap door to the cellar be removed and a handrail installed by the steps. He also had them put in two rooms with a small shared bathroom, widening the pit Carlos Argentino Daneri had once used as a darkroom. Two barred windows at street level let in the light and air. Since 1970, the only occupant of the cellar, said Enriqueta, is Don Sesostris Bonorino, an employee of the Monserrat Municipal Library, who does not tolerate visitors. She'd never known him to have company. Years ago, he had two feisty cats, tall and agile as mastiffs, who scared the rats away. One summer morning, when he went to work, he left the windows half open and some swine threw a fish fillet soaked in poison into the cellar. You can imagine what the poor man found when he came home: the cats were on top of a cushion of papers, swollen and stiff. Since then he keeps himself busy writing an encyclopedia of the nation that he can never finish. The floor and walls are covered with index cards and notations, and who knows how he manages to go to the bathroom or sleep, because there are index cards all over the bed too. As long as I can remember, no one's ever cleaned that place.

And he alone is the owner of the alé? asked El Tucumano.

The aleph has no owner, I said. No one's ever seen it.

Bonorino's seen it, Enriqueta corrected me. Sometimes he copies onto the index cards what he remembers, although I think he gets the stories mixed up.

Grete and her friends insisted on going down to the cellar to see if the aleph radiated some aura or signal. Beyond the third step, however, access was blocked by Bonorino's index cards. One of the tourists, who looked exactly like Björk, was so frustrated that she stomped back to the bus, not wanting to see anything else.

The conversations in the lobby, Grete's tale and the brief walk through the ruins of the house, where a few fragments of the old parquet floor still coexisted with the predominant cement and two or three original handcrafted mouldings, which Enriqueta now used as ornaments, plus the interminable questions about the aleph, had all taken almost forty minutes instead of the ten anticipated in the itinerary.

The tour guide was waiting with her hands on her hips by the door to the boarding house while the bus driver hurried them up with rude blasts of the horn. El Tucumano told me to keep Grete back and ask her if the group was interested in seeing the aleph.

How am I going to say that? I protested. There is no aleph. And anyhow, Bonorino's there.

You do what I tell you. If they want to see it, I'll arrange the show for them at ten. It'll be fifteen pesos each, tell them.

I gave in and obeyed. Grete wanted to know if it would be worth it and I answered that I didn't know. In any case, they were busy that night, she said. They were being taken to hear tangos at the Casa Blanca and then to the Vuelta de Rocha, a kind of bay that formed in the Riachuelo, almost at its mouth, where they hoped a singer whose name they'd refused to divulge would be performing.

It'll be Martel, I guessed.

I said so, although I knew it wasn't possible, because Martel didn't respond to any other laws but those of the secret map he was drawing. Perhaps the Vuelta de Rocha was on that map, I thought. Perhaps he only chose places where there was already a story, or where there soon would be. Until I'd heard him sing, I couldn't prove it.

I only want to remember what I've never seen, Martel had said that very afternoon, according to what I was later told by Alcira Villar, the woman who'd fallen in love with him when she heard him sing in El Rufián bookstore and who would stay with him till his death. For Martel, remembering was the same as invoking, Alcira told me, recovering what the past put out of reach, which is what he did with the lyrics of the lost tangos.

Though not a real beauty, Alcira was incredibly attractive. More than once, when we met to talk in La Paz café, I noticed men turning to look at her, trying to fix in their memories the strangeness of her face, which had nothing special about it except an unusual charm that made people stop. She was tall and tanned, with thick dark hair and black inquisitive eyes, like Sonia Braga in *The Kiss of the Spider Woman*. From the moment I met her I envied her voice, grave and sure of itself, and her long, elegant fingers, which moved slowly, as if requesting permission. I never dared ask how she could have fallen in love with Martel, who was almost an invalid and devoid of charm. It's shocking how many women prefer intelligent conversation to solid muscles.

As well as being seductive, Alcira was selfless. Although she worked eight to ten hours a day as a freelance researcher for publishers of technical books and news magazines, she spent the rest of her time being a devoted nurse to Martel, who behaved – she herself would later tell me – erratically, childishly, sometimes begging her never to leave his side, then paying her no attention for days at a time, treating her as if she were a misfortune.

Alcira had done some research for books and leaflets written about the Waterworks Palace, completed in 1894, on Córdoba Avenue. She had learned about the details of the baroque structure thought up by Belgian, Norwegian and English architects. The exterior design was by Olaf Boye – she told me – a friend of Ibsen's who met him every afternoon in the Grand Café in Christiania to play chess. They would sit there for hours without speaking, and in the intervals between one move and the next, Boye completed the arabesques for his ambitious project while Ibsen was writing *The Master Builder*.

At that time, engineering works located in residential areas of cities would have the outsides of the buildings wrapped in sculpted designs to hide the ugliness of the machines. The more complex and utilitarian the inside, the more elaborate the exterior should be. Boye had been entrusted with encasing the pipes, tanks and siphons that would supply Buenos Aires with water in limestone mosaics, cast iron caryatids, marble plaques, terracotta tiled roofs, doors and windows with so many carved folds and glazes that each of the details was rendered invisible in the jungle of colours and shapes that overwhelmed the façade. The function of the building was to cover what was inside behind so many scrolls that it disappeared, but also the sight from outside was so unbelievable that the inhabitants of the city had finally forgotten that the palace, intact for more than a century, still existed.

Alcira took Martel in his wheelchair to the corner of Córdoba and Ayacucho, where he could see that one of the attic roofs, the southeastern one, had a slight lean, just a couple of centimeters, perhaps due to the architect's momentary distraction or because the angle of the street produced this optical illusion. The sky, which had been crystalline all morning, turned a leaden grey at two in the afternoon. A thin fog drifted up from the sidewalk, warning of the drizzle that was ready to start falling at any moment, and it was impossible to know – Alcira told me – if it was cold or hot, because the humidity created a deceptive temperature, which sometimes felt suffocating and then, a few minutes later, chilled you to the bone. This obliged the inhabitants of Buenos Aires to dress not according to what the thermometers revealed but to what the radio and television stations mentioned all the time as the 'thermo-sensation factor,' which depended on the barometric pressure and wind direction.

Even at the risk of the impending rain, Martel insisted on observing the palace from the sidewalk and stayed there, absorbed, for ten or fifteen minutes, turning to Alcira every once in a while to ask: Are you sure this marvel is only a shell to hide the water? To which she replied: There is no water anymore. Only the tanks and pipes for long-departed water are left.

Boye had altered the plans hundreds of times, Alcira told me, because as the capital grew, the government ordered tanks and pools of greater capacity, which required sounder metal structures and deeper cement foundations. The more water that was to be distributed, the more pressure was needed, which meant the tanks had to be raised in a perfectly flat city whose only slope was the banks of the Río de la Plata. More than once it was suggested to Boye that he neglect the harmony of style and resign himself to an eclectic palace, like so many other buildings in Buenos

Aires, but the architect demanded that the rigorous French Renaissance symmetry of the original plans be respected.

The associates of the firm Bateman, Parsons & Bateman, in charge of the work, were still dismantling and reassembling the iron skeleton of the plumbing, in a frenzied race with the voracious expansion of the city, when Boye decided to return to Christiania. From the table he shared with Ibsen in the Grand Café he sent the drawings of the pieces that would make up the façade by post, which took a week to get to London, where they were approved, before traveling on to Buenos Aires. Since almost every piece was drawn to scale, and placing one anywhere other than its specified destination could have disastrous consequences for the symmetry of the whole, it was imperative that the designer – whose sketches numbered more than two thousand – have the precision of a player able to dominate several simultaneous games of chess blindfolded. Boye was not only concerned with the beauty of the decorations, which represented botanical images, crests of the provinces of Argentina and fantastical zoological figures, but also with the materials each one should be made from and the quality of the enamels. Sometimes it was difficult to follow his directions, which were written in tiny letters – and in English – at the bottom of the drawings, because the architect expanded on the details of the grain of the marble from Azul, the temperature the ceramics should be fired at and the chisels that should be used to cut the pieces of granite. Boye died of a heart attack, in the middle of a game of chess, on the 10th of October 1892, when he had yet to complete the sketches for the southeast attic roof. Bateman, Parsons & Bateman assigned the task of finishing the last details to one of its technical draughtsmen, but a defect in the granite used for the base of the southeastern tower, in addition to the last eighty-six terracotta tiles being broken on the voyage from England, delayed the construction and produced the almost imperceptible deviation in the symmetry that Martel noticed the afternoon of his visit.

On the top floor of the palace, overlooking Riobamba Street, the water company has a small museum where it exhibits some of Boye's drawings, as well as the original chlorine ejectors, valves, lengths of pipe, late nineteenth-century sanitation fixtures and scale models showing how Bateman and Boye had tried, unsuccessfully, to make their palace into something useful to Buenos Aires but, at the same time, something which would somehow become unfaithful to the city's lost grandeur. Since Martel insisted on seeing the most insignificant traces of that past before going up to the monstrous galleries and tanks that took up almost the whole of the interior of the building, Alcira pushed his wheelchair up the ramp leading to the entrance hall, where customers still paid their water bills at a string of windows, at the end of which was the entrance to the museum.

Martel was dazzled by the virtually translucent china of the lavatories and bidets on display in the two adjoining rooms, and by the enamel of the moldings and sheets of terracotta displayed on felt-covered pedestals, as shiny as the day they'd come out of the kiln. Some of Boye's drawings were framed, and others were kept in rolls. Two of them had notes by Ibsen about the play he was writing. Alcira had copied a phrase, *De tok av Forbindingene uken etter*, which maybe meant 'They removed the bandages after a week,' and chess annotations indicating the moment the match was interrupted. Martel replied to each of his companion's explanations with the same phrase: 'God, imagine that! The very hand that wrote *A Doll's House!*'

It was impossible to get up to the interior galleries by wheelchair, much less pass along the narrow aisles that overlooked the great interior patio, fenced in by one hundred and eighty cast iron columns. None of those obstacles intimidated the singer, who seemed possessed by an *idée fixe*. 'I've got to get up there, Alcirita,' he said. Perhaps he was driven by the idea that some of the hundreds of workers – who labored for sixteen hours a day on the construction of the palace, not even having Sundays off or lunch breaks, spending their brief nights in brothels or tenements – would have whistled or hummed on the scaffolding the first of the city's tangos, the real ones, because they knew no other happiness than that produced by that hesitant music. Or maybe, as Alcira believed, what motivated him was a curiosity to see the little tank in the southeast corner, under the attic skylight, which could have been used to store water in times of extreme drought or as a place to deposit unusable bits of pipe. After studying the plans of the palace, Colonel Moori Koenig had chosen that cubicle to hide the mummy of Evita Perón in 1955, after taking her away from the embalmer, Pedro Ara, but an uncontrollable fire in the neighboring houses prevented him when he was very close to achieving his objective. In the same place, more than a hundred years earlier, a crime so atrocious had been committed that it was still spoken of in Buenos Aires, where unpunished crimes abound.

Each time Martel got out of his wheelchair and decided to walk with crutches he ran the risk of tearing a muscle and suffering another of his painful internal hemorrhages. That afternoon, however, since he had an urgent need to climb those sinuous iron staircases to get to the highest tanks, he gathered his patience and hoisted the weight of his body from one step to the next, while Alcira, behind him, carrying the crutches, prayed he wouldn't fall on top of her. He rested every little while and, after some deep breaths, tackled the next steps, with his neck veins swollen and his pigeon's chest about to explode beneath his shirt. Even when Alcira tried to dissuade him over and over again, thinking how the torment would be repeated on the way down, the singer carried on as if possessed. When they got to the top, almost entirely out of breath, he collapsed on one of the iron girders and remained there, eyes closed, for several minutes until the blood returned to its course. But when he opened his eyes his astonishment left him breathless again. What he saw surpassed the oneiric sets from *Metropolis*. Ceramic necking, lintels, tiny blinds, valves, the premises as a whole gave the impression of the nest of a monstrous animal. The water had long disappeared from the twelve tanks divided between three levels, but the memory of the water was still there, with its silent metamorphoses as it entered the pumping station's pipes and the dangerous swells that disfigured it at the slightest onslaught of the winds. The reserve tanks, located in the four attics, were especially susceptible to falling, when the southeasterly whipped up, breaking the subtle balance of the pillars, the horizontal panels and the valves.

The pink water of the river gradually changed as it flowed from one canal to the next, detaching itself in the locks from the urine, semen, scandals of the city and frenzies of the birds, purifying itself of the savage past, life's toxins, and returning to the transparency of its origins until eventually cloistering itself in those tanks criss-crossed by streamers and joists, but awake, even in memory, always awake, because water was the only thing that could find its way through the ins and outs of that labyrinth.

The central patio, which Boye earmarked for public baths, but the overblown construction of which had reduced to an area of three hundred square meters, was covered in mosaics whose extravagant designs obsessively imitated the geometry of kaleidoscopes. At that time of the afternoon when the light coming in through the skylights hit them directly, vapors of colors more vivid even than rainbows rose from the floor, forming shimmering arcs that broke up when the slightest sound vibrated in the cavern. Martel went over to one of the banisters that separated the tanks from the abyss and sang: *Aaaaaaa*. The colors waved madly, and the echo of the sleeping metals repeated the vowel infinitely: *aaaaaaaa*.

Then, he stood up so straight and tall that he resembled another being, handsome and supple. Alcira thought some miracle had restored him to health. His hair, which Martel always combed with brilliantine, slicking it down and straightening it to look like that of his idol Carlos Gardel, sprang up in rebellious ringlets. His face was transfigured by an astounded expression that conveyed both beatitude and wildness, as if the palace had put a spell on him.

I heard him sing an other-worldly song then – Alcira told me – with a voice that seemed to contain thousands of other bereaved voices. It must have been an antediluvian tango, because he phrased it in a language even less comprehensible than that of the works in his repertoire; it was more like phonetic sparks, random sounds in which you could detect feelings like sorrow, desertion, lamented lost happiness, homesickness, to which only Martel's voice could give any meaning. What do *brenai, ayaúú, panísola* mean? Because that was more or less what he sang. I felt that it wasn't just one person's past flowing through that music, but all those pasts the city had witnessed as far back in time as you could go, to the time when it was just useless scrubland.

The song lasted two or three minutes. Martel was exhausted when he finished it, and struggled back to the iron girder. There had been some subtle change in the premises. The immense tanks still reflected, now very quietly, the last waves of the voice, and the radiance from the skylights brushed the damp mosaics of the patio and lifted smoky figures as distinct as snowflakes. It wasn't those variations that caught Alcira's attention, however, but an unexpected awakening of the objects. Was the handle of some valve turning? Was it possible that the water, though cut off since

1915, was stretching in the locks? Things like that never happen, she told herself. Nevertheless, the door of the tank in the southeast corner, sealed by the rust of its hinges, was now ajar and a milky brightness marked the fissure. The singer stood up, driven by another flow of energy, and walked towards the place. I pretended to lean on him so he would lean on me, Alcira told me months later. It was me who opened the door all the way, she said. A stench of death and damp took my breath away. There was something in the tank, but we didn't see anything. Outside it was covered by a decorative mansard, with two skylights letting in the three o'clock afternoon sun. From the floor, as shiny as if no one had ever touched it, rose the same mist we'd seen in other parts of the palace. But the silence was thicker there: so absolute you could almost touch it. Neither Martel nor I dared speak, although we were both thinking then what we didn't say out loud till we'd left the building: that the door of the tank had been opened by the ghost of the adolescent who'd been tortured in that space a century before.

The disappearance of Felicitas Alcántara happened on the last afternoon of 1899. She'd just turned fourteen and had already been a famous beauty since childhood. Tall, with an indolent manner, she had astonishing iridescent eyes, which instantly poisoned anyone who looked into them with inevitable love. Many had asked for her hand in matrimony, but her parents felt she was worthy only of a prince. At the end of the nineteenth century princes didn't come to Buenos Aires. It would be twenty-five years yet before

Umberto of Savoy, Edward Windsor and the Maharaja of Kapurtala appeared. The Alcántaras lived, therefore, in voluntary seclusion. Their Bourbon residence, in San Isidro, on the banks of the Río de la Plata, was adorned, like the Waterworks Palace, with four towers covered in slate and tortoiseshell. They were so ostentatious that on clear days they could be seen from the coast of Uruguay.

On December 31st, just after one in the afternoon, Felicitas and her four younger sisters were cooling off in the yellow water of the river. The family's governesses were all French. There were too many of them and they didn't know the customs of the country. To keep themselves occupied they wrote letters home or talked of their romantic disappointments while the girls disappeared from view, in the reed beds by the beach. From the stoves in the house came aromas of the turkeys and suckling pigs roasting for the midnight meal. In the cloudless sky birds flew in untidy gusts, pecking at each other viciously. One of the governesses commented that in the village she came from in Gascony there was no worse omen than the wrath of birds.

At one-thirty, the girls were supposed to go home for their siesta. When the governesses called them, Felicitas did not appear. They could see a few sailboats on the horizon and clouds of butterflies over the stiff, scorched puddles. For a long time the governesses searched in vain. They weren't afraid she'd drowned, because she was a strong swimmer who knew all the river's tricks. Boats filled with fruits and vegetables passed by on their way back from the markets and, from the shore, the desperate women shouted to them asking if they'd seen a distracted girl in the deeper waters upstream. No one paid them any attention. They'd all been celebrating the new year since first thing and were rowing drunkenly. Three quarters of an hour went by.

That loss of time was fatal, because Felicitas didn't appear that day or the following ones, and her parents always believed that if they'd been informed straight away, they would have found a trail. Before dawn on January 1st 1900, several police patrols were combing the region from the islands of the Tigre Delta all the way down to the banks of Belgrano, marring the summer tranquility. The search was under the command of the ferocious colonel and commissioner, Ramón L. Falcón, who would become famous in 1909 when he dispersed the crowd gathered in Plaza Lorea to protest the electoral fraud. Eight people died in the skirmish and another sixteen were gravely injured. Six months later, the young Russian anarchist Simon Radowitzky, who had miraculously emerged unscathed, blew the commissioner up in revenge by throwing a bomb into his carriage as it passed. Radowitzky expiated his crime for twenty-one years in the Ushuahia prison. Falcón is today immortalized by a marble statue two blocks from the scene of the attack.

The commissioner was known for his resolve and perspicacity. None of the cases he'd been assigned had ever been left unsolved, until the disappearance of Felicitas Alcántara. When no guilty party was available, he'd invent one. But on this occasion he lacked suspects, a body and even an explicable crime. There was a single obvious motive that no one dared mention: the disturbing beauty of the victim. A few boaters thought they'd seen, on the last afternoon of the year, a well-built, older man with large ears and a handlebar moustache, scouring the beaches with binoculars from a rowboat. One of them said the onlooker had two enormous warts beside his nose, but no one attached much importance to this claim, since Colonel Falcón had precisely the same identifying marks.

Buenos Aires was then such a splendid city that Julet Huret, correspondent for *Le Figaro*, wrote that when he disembarked it reminded him of London with its narrow streets lined with benches, Vienna with its two-horse carriages and Paris with its wide sidewalks and terrace cafés. The central avenues were lit with incandescent lamps that often exploded when someone passed by. They were excavating tunnels for the subway system. Two lines of electrified streetcars circulated from Ministro Inglés Street to the Portones de Palermo and from the Plaza de Mayo to Retiro Station. The racket cracked the foundations of some houses and made their residents think the end of the world was nigh. The capital opened the doors of its palaces to its illustrious visitors. The most praised was the Waterworks, in spite of how, according to the poet Rubén Darío, it imitated the sick imagination of Ludwig II of Bavaria. Until 1902, the palace was unguarded. Since the only treasure in the place were the water galleries and there was no danger of anyone robbing them, the government considered paying for security a useless expense. The disappearance of some terracotta decorations imported from England resulted in security guards being hired.

Buenos Aires' water was extracted by huge siphons in the river a mile off the coast of the neighborhood of Belgrano, and taken through underwater tunnels to deposits in Palermo, where the excrement was filtered out and salts and chlorine added. After the purification, a network of pipes propelled it towards the palace on Córdoba Avenue. Commissioner Falcón ordered all the pipes to be drained and checked for evidence, which left the poorer quarters of the city without water that torrid February of 1900.

Months passed with no news of Felicitas. In early 1901 pamphlets appeared before the Alcántaras' front door with insidious messages about the victim's fate. None gave the slightest clue. *La Felicidad was a virgin. Not anymore*, said one. And another, more perverse: *Ride Felicitas for a peso in the whorehouse at 2300 Junín Street*. That address does not exist.

The adolescent's body was discovered one morning in April of 1901, when the night watchman arrived at the Waterworks Palace to clean the living space assigned to him and his family in the southeast wing of the palace. The girl was covered in a light tunic of river grasses and her mouth was full of round pebbles that turned to dust when they fell to the ground. Contrary to what the authorities had specu- lated, she was as immaculate as the day she came into the world. Her beautiful eyes were frozen in an expression of astonishment, and the only sign of mistreatment was a dark line around her neck left by the guitar string used to strangle her. Beside the corpse were the remains of a fire the murderer must have lit and a fine linen handkerchief of a no-longer identifiable color, with the still discernible initials RLF. The news of the initials was profoundly upsetting to Commissioner Falcón, because those were his initials and it was a given that the handkerchief belonged to the guilty party. Till the end of his days he maintained that the kidnapping and murder of Felicitas Alcántara was an act of vengeance against him, and came up with the impossible hypothesis that the girl had been taken by boat to the deposit in Palermo, strangled there and dragged through the pipes to the palace on Córdoba Street. Falcón never ventured a word on the motives of the crime, even less fathomable once sex and money were ruled out.

Shortly after Felicitas' body was found, the Alcántaras sold their property and emigrated to France. The security guards refused to occupy the apartment in the southeast rectangle of the Waterworks Palace, choosing instead the wooden house the government offered them on the banks of the Riachuelo, in one of the most insalubrious areas of the city. At the end of 1915, the President of the Republic personally ordered the wretched rooms to be closed, sealed and removed from the public records, which is why on all the diagrams of the palace subsequent to that date there appears an irregular space, which is still attributed to a construction error. In Argentina there is now a secular custom of suppressing from history all the facts that contradict the official ideas of the grandeur of the country. There are no impure heroes or lost wars. The canonical books of the nineteenth century pride themselves on the disappearance of the blacks from Buenos Aires, without taking into consideration that in the records of 1840 a quarter of the population still declared themselves black or mulatto. With a similar intention, Borges wrote in 1972 that people remembered Evita only because the newspapers kept committing the stupid error of mentioning her. It's understandable, then, even if the southeast corner of the Waterworks Palace could be seen from the street, people would say the place didn't exist.

Alcira's tale made me think that the Alcántara girl and Evita summoned up the same sort of resistance, one for her beauty, the other for her power. In the girl, beauty was intolerable because it gave her power; in Evita, power was intolerable because it gave her recognition. Both their lives were so excessive that, like the inconvenient facts of history, they were left without a real place of their own. Only in novels could they find the place they belonged, as always happens in Argentina to people who have the arrogance to exist too much.

THREE

November 2001

The boarding house was silent during the day and noisy at night, when the tenants of the room next door became embroiled in their interminable fights and the kids started screaming. I resigned myself, therefore, to writing my dissertation elsewhere. Every day, from one in the morning till six, I was at a table in the Café Británico, across from Parque Lezama. It was just a few steps from my riotous dwelling and it never closed. Sometimes I whiled away the hours contemplating the shadows of the ruined gardens through the filleted windows and the benches now occupied by homeless families. On one of those benches, in the spring of 1944, Borges had kissed Estela Canto for the first time. Though ashamed of his uncontrollable ardor the previous day he'd sent her a passionate love letter: *I am in Buenos Aires, I shall see you tonight, I shall see you tomorrow, I know we shall be happy together (happy and drifting and sometimes speechless and most gloriously silly)*. Borges was forty-five years old then, but he expressed his feelings with clumsy terror. That night he'd kissed Estela on one of the benches and then kissed and embraced her again in the amphitheater off

Brasil Street, opposite the cupolas of the Russian Orthodox Church.

Hugo Wast, a rabid Catholic novelist, who had just been named Minister of Justice, decided to censure everything the Vatican considered immoral – the idea of sex, in the first instance – because he believed that therein lay the origins of Argentine decadence. He went after the tango viciously, ordering obscene lyrics to be replaced by more pious ones, and sent Buenos Aires policemen out to hunt down couples who touched each other in the streets.

Borges and Estela were easy prey. In the lonely moonlit amphitheater, their embracing silhouettes were conspicuously eye-catching. An officer from Station 14 suddenly appeared before them, 'as if he'd fallen out of the sky,' Estela would later say, and asked for their identity papers. They'd both forgotten them. He arrested them and left them sitting in a patio, with other vagabonds, until three in the morning.

I learned this story from Sesostris Bonorino, who knew even the tiniest details. Only later did I imagine where he'd got them. He knew that Estela had a packet of Condal cigarettes in her handbag that night and that she'd smoked two of the nine that were left; he could describe the contents of the pockets of Borges' jacket: a pen, two candies, several rust-coloured one-peso bills, and a piece of paper on which he'd written a line from Yeats: *I'm looking for the face I had / Before the world was made*.

One night, when I was leaving for the Café Británico, I heard someone calling me from the cellar. Bonorino was kneeling on the fourth or fifth step, sticking index cards on the banister. He was squat and bald as an onion, with no neck and shoulders raised so high it was hard to tell whether he had a backpack on or was a hunchback. Not long before, seeing him in the light of day, I'd been shocked by his yellow, almost translucent coloring. He seemed affable, and treated me with deference, perhaps because I was there temporarily and because I shared his passion for books. He asked if I'd lend him a book for a few hours, *Through the Labyrinth*, the thick volume edited by Prestel I'd brought in my luggage.

I don't need to read it, because I already know everything it says, he bragged. I just want to study the figures.

I was quite taken aback and it was several seconds before I could even answer him. No one had seen Prestel's book, which remained unopened in my suitcase. It also seemed improbable that he could have read it, since it had been published less than a year earlier in London and New York. Furthermore, he pronounced each letter of the word *Through* as if it were a Spanish word. I wondered whether Enriqueta, when she cleaned my room, also went through my things.

How nice to have a neighbor who speaks English, I said in English. From his indifferent expression, I surmised he hadn't understood a word.

I'm preparing a National Encyclopedia, he answered. If you wouldn't mind, I'd appreciate if you could tell me about some of the Anglo-Saxon working methods one of these days. I've heard a lot about Oxford and Webster's, but I'm not able to read them. I know more things than a normal man of my age knows, but what I've learned is what no one teaches.

What use would Prestel's book be to you, then? The labyrinths in there are designed to confuse, not to clarify.

I'm not so sure. For me, they're paths that don't allow one to retreat, or a way of moving without ever leaving the same spot. When we see the image of a labyrinth we think, erroneously, that its shape comes from the lines that draw it. It's the opposite: the shape is in the blank spaces between these lines. Will you lend me the vade mecum?

Of course, I said. I'll bring it down to you tomorrow.

I would have gone back up to my room to get it, but I'd arranged to meet El Tucumano at the Británico at one-thirty and I was already late. Since we'd met the Scandinavians, my friend had been obsessed with setting up an aleph show for tourists in the cellar and he needed to get Bonorino either out of the way or on board. The venture seemed ludicrous to me, but I was in fact the one who finally found the solution. The librarian was fanatical about order, and he'd notice if any one of his index cards had been moved. Beyond the fifth step, the little square cards, of varying colors and sizes, formed a spiderweb the design of which only he knew. If anyone so much as brushed one of them with their foot on the way down the steps, Bonorino would cry to the heavens and run off to get the police. El Tucumano had tried to approach the cellar several times without success. I, on the other hand, had managed to capture the old man's interest by showing him an anthology I had with me, *Índice de la nueva poesía americana*, which contained three poems by Borges that had never appeared anywhere else: 'The Guitar,' 'To Serrano Street' and 'Dusk,' and the first version of '*Dulcia linquimus arva.*' I imagined a scholar like Bonorino wouldn't be able to resist the temptation of seeing how Borges gradually got rid of rhetorical impurities as he progressed from one draft to the next.

I waited for El Tucumano in the reserved room of the café. I liked to make out the silhouette of the palms and tipa trees in the Parque Lezama from there, and to imagine the great masonry urns in the Central Avenue, on clay pedestals with identical bas-reliefs depicting the goddess of fertility. The place was hostile in the early hours and no one dared walk through it. For me it was enough to know it was on the other side of the street. That park was the birthplace of Buenos Aires and spread out from its slopes over flat countryside, defying the ferocity of the southeasterlies and the voracious river mud. At night it felt more humid there than in other parts of the city, and people were stifled in the summer and chilled to the bone in winter. The Británico, however, managed to make it imperceptible.

In the middle of October the weather had been good, and I'd lost many hours of work listening to the waiter tell of the times of patriotic fervor, during the Falklands war, when the café had to call itself the Tánico, and enumerate the times Borges had stopped in for a glass of sherry, and Ernesto Sabato had sat at the very table I was occupying at that moment to write the first pages of his novel *On Heroes and Tombs*. I knew the waiter's stories were mythologies for foreigners, and that Sabato didn't have to go so far away to write when he had a comfortable studio in Santos Lugares, outside the city limits, with a huge library to which he could turn when he needed inspiration. Just in case, I never sat at that table again.

El Tucumano arrived half an hour late. I never went anywhere without my copy of *Índice* – for which any used book dealer would have paid five hundred dollars at that time – and a couple of books of postcolonial theory, with which I planned to analyse the concept of the nation by way of the tangos Borges mentioned. During the first few hours after midnight, however, my attention flew off in any direction, be it the Quilmes Cristal bottles or the double gins customers ordered, or the flank attack on the black king on the chessboard where two solitary old men battled. I emerged from my distraction when El Tucumano put a spherical prop in front of my eyes; it was about the size of a ping-pong ball, like a Christmas tree ornament. The surface was covered in tiny mirrors, some of them colored, and it sparkled in the lamplight.

The alé is more or less like this, no? he said with a swagger.

Perhaps it might be a good decoy for the unwary. Certain details fit Borges' narration: it was a small iridescent sphere, however, its brilliance wasn't intolerable.

More or less, I answered. We tourists will swallow any old baloney.

I tried playing around with Buenos Aires' subterranean lexicon, but what came naturally to El Tucumano confused me. Sometimes, in the reflections I wrote for my thesis, one or another of these fleeting words would slip out. I'd get rid of it as soon as I noticed, because when I returned to Manhattan I would have forgotten them. The language of Buenos Aires shifted so quickly that the words appeared first and then reality arrived, and the words carried on when reality had already left.

According to El Tucumano, an electrician could illuminate the sphere from within or, even better, train a ray of halogen light on it to give a certain spectral appearance. I suggested that to increase the dramatic effect he could play a cassette of Borges listing what he saw in the aleph in his unsteady voice. He loved the idea:

See that, beastie? If it wasn't for Don Sexotrix, we could be making a killing, we'd break Buenos Aires.

I couldn't get used to El Tucumano calling me beastie, tiger, titan. I preferred the more affectionate names that sometimes slipped out when it was just the two of us. It didn't happen very often, only when I begged him or showered him with gifts. Almost all our private moments were lost in discussions of strategies to exploit the false aleph, which El Tucumano, for some reason, saw as a brilliant business opportunity.

The following night I went to the cellar with the Prestel volume in hand. Standing by the banister, Bonorino was taking notes in an enormous notebook, the kind they use for accounts. I saw him copy a few phrases onto the colored index cards, which were piled on the second and third step: the green rectangles on the left, the yellow rhomboids in the middle, the red squares on the right. 'I have in mind,' he said, 'the route of the Lacroze streetcar from Constitución to Cabildo, in 1930. The vehicles left the station and then went past the sleepy houses of the south, along Santiago del Estero Street, and Pozos, and Entre Ríos. Only when it reached the Almagro neighborhood did it veer off to the north, then covered in vegetable patches and vacant lots. It was another city, I've seen it.'

I kept admiring that display of topographical erudition, while Bonorino, pencil in hand, feverishly wrote down the route. I would have liked to verify if everything he said was true. I made a note in the book by John King I had with me: 'Lacroze, line 4. Bonor. says streetcars were white with green stripe.' The librarian poured what he knew out onto the index cards, but I could never figure out what his classification criteria were, what information went with which color.

For several minutes, with the Prestel open, I talked to him about the intricate mandalas outlined in the floors of French cathedrals: Amiens, Mirepoix and especially Chartres. He replied that the ones we had in front of our noses and let pass unnoticed were more fascinating. Since the conversation was going on for longer than I'd expected, I had the providential idea of inviting him to come to the Británico for a cup of tea, knowing he never went out. He scratched his bald head and asked me if I'd mind having it down there, in his little kitchen.

I instantly accepted, although I felt a twinge of guilt for delaying that night's reading. When I got to the third step down to the cellar, I realized I couldn't go any further. The cards were spread out all over the place, in such a strange order that they seemed alive and capable of imperceptible movements. Please, wait till I turn out the light, said Bonorino. Although the only lamp that illuminated the space was a twenty-five-watt bulb, further dimmed by the fly shit that covered it, the absence of that light was enough to make the stairs disappear completely. I felt a boneless hand take me by the elbow, dragging me downwards. I say dragging and I'm mistaken, because in reality I floated, weightless, while I heard around me a crackling that must have been the cards moving out of my way.

The librarian's dwelling was miserable. Since the windows at street level were permanently shut since the episode with the cats, it was almost impossible to breathe. I'm sure that if someone were to try and light a match it would have gone straight out. I saw a shelf with ten or twelve books, among which I distinguished the Sopena thesaurus and a biography of Yrigoyen by Manuel Gálvez. The walls were covered from floor to ceiling with greasy papers, stuck one on top of the other like the pages of an almanac. There I saw drawings that perfectly reproduced the inner workings of a Stradivarius, or indicated how high voltage electricity was distributed from an iron nucleus, or duplicated a Querandí mask, or imitated systems of writing I'd never seen or imagined. They seemed like dispersed fragments of an endless dictionary.

I carefully observed his lair while Bonorino was busy leafing through Prestel's thick volume. Over and over again I heard him say, looking at the drawing of the city of Jericho trapped in a labyrinth of ramparts and the mysterious Swedish labyrinth of Ytterholmen, this meaningless phrase: 'If I want to get to the center I must not leave the edge, if I want to walk to the edge I cannot move from the center.'

Besides being shut up, the cellar was covered in films of dust that were stirred by the slightest provocation. At one end, beneath the window, I saw a dilapidated bedstead with a blanket of some indiscernible color. A shirt or two hung from nails in the few spots that hadn't been invaded by the notes; beside the bed, two fruit crates served, perhaps, as stools or nightstands. The little bathroom had no door and consisted of a toilet and a sink, where Bonorino must have got all his water from because the kitchen area, smaller than a cupboard, had only a board and a gas camp stove.

Bonorino's language contradicted his asceticism: it was florid, elliptical and, most of all, evasive. I never managed to get him to respond to my questions directly. When I wanted to know how he'd come to be living in the boarding house, he gave me a long sermon on poverty. With great difficulty I discovered the previous owner had been an arthritic Bulgarian aristocrat, to whom Bonarino read in the evenings from the few novels he got from the Monserrat library. I deduced this from a myriad of phrases among which I remember, because I wrote it down: 'I had to skip from the felonies of Monsieur Danglars and Caderousse and didn't stop until Inspector Javert fell into the mud of the Seine.' I asked him if this meant he'd read *The Count of Monte Cristo* and *Les Misérables* in one sitting, impossible feats even for the insomniac teenager I'd been, and he answered with another riddle: 'Nothing hard lasts forever.'

While we talked, I noticed that the floor underneath the bottom step was clean and clear, and I imagined that Bonorino often lay down there, flat on his back, as Borges' story decreed. I assumed that this was how he contemplated the aleph and I felt, I confess, a despicable envy. It seemed unfair that this Quasimodo of a librarian had appropriated an object we all had a right to see.

The tea we drank was cold and after fifteen minutes of conversation I was fainting with boredom. Bonorino, though, was chatting away with enthusiasm, the way lonely people do. Patiently, I gradually plucked a few interesting facts from his luxuriant loquacity. That's how I found out he'd never paid a cent for the hovel, so it would be easy to get him evicted. No one coveted the basement room, because it was an unhealthy cell, suitable only for storing tools and beverages. But if the aleph was still in that place, then it was worth more than the building, more than the whole block, and maybe as much as Buenos Aires, since it held all that the city was, is and would be. However, although I mentioned Borges' story again and again, Bonorino avoided the subject and preferred to admire the beauty of the Seaver passage, remembering the gentle slope, the slate-roofed houses, the steps that went up to Posadas Street. He suggested we go for a walk there some time and I didn't dare tell him the passage had disappeared decades before, when 9 de Julio Avenue was extended as far as the walls of Retiro.

I got to the Café Británico at two-thirty in the morning. Six or seven tables were occupied, double the usual number at that hour. I saw the regular chess players, a couple of actors on their way back from the theater and a failed songwriter who was tuning individual chords on his guitar. I noticed they were all moving nervously, like birds on the eve of an earthquake, but neither I nor anybody else would have been able to say why at that moment.

That night I made very little progress on my thesis and, when I realized it was all coming out badly, I tried to read a few books on postcolonial theory, but I couldn't even concentrate enough to take notes. I couldn't keep the idea of getting Bonorino out of the way so El Tucumano could set up his show out of my head. Although I did almost everything El Tucumano asked of me, what I really wanted was to have the cellar to myself. In my flashes of rationality, I realized the existence of the aleph was illusory. It was one of Borges' fictions, which took place in a building that had been demolished over half a century ago. 'I'm going crazy,' I said, 'I've got a screw loose.'

I shoved the idea away and it came straight back. Even against all notions of reality, I believed the aleph was below the last step of the cellar and that, if I lay down in a supine position on the floor, I'd be able to see it the way Bonorino saw it. Without the aleph, the librarian wouldn't have been able to draw the inside of a Stradivarius with such precision or reproduce the moment when Borges and Estela Canto kissed in the Parque Lezama. It was an indestructible sphere fixed in a single point in the universe. If the boarding house was struck by lightning or Buenos Aires ceased to exist, the point would still be there, perhaps invisible to those who didn't know how to see it but no less real for that. Borges had been able to forget. I was tirelessly tormented by it.

Until then my days had been routine and happy. In the afternoons I sat in the cafés and visited second-hand book-stores; in one of them I found a first edition of *The Early Italian Poets*, by Dante Gabriel Rossetti, for six dollars, and Samuel Johnson's book on Shakespeare published by Yale for a dollar fifty, because the covers were bent. Since before I arrived, unemployment was increasing unchecked and thousands of people were selling off their assets and leaving the country. Some hundred-year-old libraries were being sold by weight, and book dealers sometimes bought things without any idea of their value.

I also liked going to El Gato Negro Café, on Corrientes Street, where I was lulled by the aroma of oregano and paprika, or sitting by the window at El Foro to watch the young lawyers go past with their entourage of clerks. On Saturdays I preferred the sunny sidewalk terrace of La Biela, across from the Recoleta, where all the apt phrases that occurred to me for my dissertation were destroyed by the intrusion of mime artists and the frightening tango spectacles in the open space in front of the Church of Pilar.

Sometimes, around ten in the evening, I'd drop into La Brigada, in San Telmo. There was a market there that stayed open till late and it was old like the century we'd left behind. At the entrances, strings of Bolivian women were stationed with their colored outfits selling bags of mysterious spices that they spread out over a piece of cloth. Inside, in the maze of galleries, kiosks of toys bumped up against stalls selling buttons and lace, like in an Arab souk. The nucleus of the square was full of sides of beef hung from hooks beside heaps of kidneys, tripe and blood sausages. In no other place in the world have things kept the flavor they'd had in the past as much as in this Buenos Aires that was, however, no longer almost anything like what it once had been.

It's always difficult to find a spot in La Brigada. To demonstrate that the meat is tender, the waiters cut it with the edge of a spoon, and it's worthwhile closing your eyes as the first bite touches your tongue, because that way the pleasure cleaves to the memory and stays in it. When I didn't want to eat alone, I approached the tables of movie directors and actors and poets who congregated there, and asked if I could join them. I'd learned when it was appropriate and when not.

The heat began in November. Even the little kids who went from place to place with wheelbarrows full of old cardboard, to sell for ten centavos a kilo, got their sorrows out of their souls and whistled music so good you could lean your head back on it: the poor kids put their hands in their pockets and all they found was the good weather, which was enough to let them forget for a moment the scorching bed where they wouldn't sleep that night.

When I got to La Brigada I saw a couple of young television actors at a table near the window. Valeria was with them and, from the drawings she was sketching for them on a piece of paper, it seemed like she was explaining some tango steps. I hadn't seen her since the night of my arrival, but her face was unforgettable because she reminded me of my maternal grandmother. She greeted me with enthusiasm. I noticed she was bored and hoping someone would rescue her.

These two guys have to dance tomorrow in a film and they don't even know the difference between a *ranchera* and a *milonga*, she told me. They both nodded, as if they hadn't heard.

Take them to La Estrella or La Viruta or whatever that place is called tonight, I answered. I turned to the young men and told them: Valeria is the best. I saw her teach a bow-legged Japanese man. By three in the morning he was dancing like Fred Astaire.

She's a lot older than us, one pointed out, stupidly. Older women don't turn me on, so I can't learn this way.

Old or young, we're all the same size in bed, I said, copying Somerset Maugham or maybe Hemingway.

The conversation languished and for a few minutes Valeria tried to keep it lively by talking about *The Swamp*, an Argentine film that reminded her of the hysteria and negligence in her own family, and therefore continued to vex her. The young men, on the other hand, had left before it finished: Graciela Borges' acting was divine, but we couldn't handle so many dogs in every scene, they said. They were barking all the time, even the cinema smelled of dog shit.

They preferred *The Son of the Bride*, where they'd cried their eyes out. I hadn't seen the most recent movies and couldn't contribute. I liked works soaked in time. In Buenos Aires, just like in Manhattan, I frequented art house cinemas and film clubs, where I found wonders that no one remembered anymore. In a little room in the San Martín theater I saw in a single day *The Flight*, an Argentine gem from 1937 that was believed lost for six decades, and *Chronicle of a Lone Boy*, which was comparable to *Les Quatre cents coups*. A week later, in a series at the Malba, I discovered a short from 1961 called *Faena (Slaughter)*, which showed cattle being knocked out with hammers and then skinned alive in the slaughterhouse. I then understood the true meaning of the word barbarous and for a whole week could think of nothing else. In New York, an experience like that would have turned me into a vegetarian. In Buenos Aires it was impossible, because there was nothing to eat but beef.

Shortly after eleven, Valeria and her students asked for the bill and stood up. They had to start filming tomorrow morning at dawn, and they still needed two or three hours of practice. When they left, I was expecting nothing more from the night, but one of the little actors surprised me:

We have to go to the ends of the earth without even sleeping, *che*. The Liniers Arcades, imagine. They'd told us to be there at noon, but then they found out it was reserved. Some deformed singer got in ahead of us. That asshole, what's his name, he said, snapping his fingers.

Martel, the other matinee idol said.

Julio Martel? I asked.

That's the one. Who's ever heard of him?

He's a great singer, Valeria corrected him. The best since Gardel.

You're the only one who says that, insisted the little actor who wasn't turned on by her. No one understands what he sings.

The anxiety wouldn't let me work or sleep. For the first time fate had allowed me to anticipate the place where Martel was going to give one of his private recitals. After seeing *Faena*, I could surmise why he had chosen the arcades, three two-story buildings, with a succession of cloister-like archways at the front, the construction of which had begun on the very same day as that of the Waterworks Palace. The northern gate was used in the past for access to the slaughter lots and the old livestock market, where at daybreak they auctioned the cattle to be eaten that day. In 1978, the dictatorship had closed down and demolished the slaughterhouse. On the forty hectares they built a pharmaceutical lab and a recreation park, but the cattle still came into the adjoining market by the trailer-load, emptied into the corrals and sold by lot, at so much a kilo.

The street the arcades were on had changed its name so many times that everyone called it whatever they wanted. At the beginning of the twentieth century, when the place was known as Chicago, and the slaughtermen used only knives imported from that butchers' city, those who ventured down that street called it calle Décima. In the parish records it was inscribed as San Fernando, in memory of a medieval prince who ate nothing but beef. The auctioneers who got together behind the blue and pink chamfer of the

Oviedo bar, right across the street from the arcades, were still calling it Tellier until recently, in homage to the Frenchman, Charles Tellier, who was the first to transport frozen meat across the Atlantic. Since 1984, however, it was called Lisandro de la Torre, after the senator who exposed the illegal meat-processing monopoly.

There are no reliable maps of Buenos Aires, because the street names change from one week to the next. What one map affirms, another denies. Directions guide and at the same time disturb. For fear of getting lost, some people never go more than ten or twelve blocks away from home in their whole lives. Enriqueta, the manager of the boarding house, for example, had never been west of 9 de Julio Avenue. 'What for?' she'd said. 'Who knows what might happen to me.'

When I finished eating at La Brigada I went to the Café Británico without stopping off at my room, like I usually did. I urgently needed to revise my notes on the film *Faena* to see whether I might find something in the rituals of the slaughterhouse that could explain Martel's presence in the arcades at noon the next day. According to the short, every morning seven thousand cows and calves ascended a ramp toward death. First, they'd waded through a pool and then been hosed down to complete the washing. At the top of the ramp, a hatch shut behind them and separated them into groups of three or four. Then they were each struck a brutal hammer blow on the back of the neck by a man naked to the waist. The blow rarely missed. The animals collapsed and were almost instantly thrown two meters down onto a cement floor. That none of them felt the imminence of death was essential to the meat's tenderness. When a cow sensed danger, it would stiffen with terror and the muscles would be permeated with a bitter flavor.

As the cattle fell from the ramp, six or seven men went along wrapping their legs with a steel wire and fitting them onto a hook while a counterweight hoisted them up off the ground, head hanging down. The movements had to be swift and precise: the animals were still alive and, if they awoke from the blackout, they put up a hell of a fight. Once hung, they advanced along an endless conveyor belt, at the rate of two hundred an hour. The slaughtermen awaited them by the waterwheel, with their knives raised: the sure point in the jugular and that was it. The blood gushed out into a canal where it would coagulate for later use. What happened next was atrocious and it seemed unthinkable to me that Martel would want to sing to that past. The cows were skinned, slit open, disembowelled and handed over, now headless and legless, to the quartermen, who chopped them in half or in pieces.

That's how it was in 1848 as well, when Esteban Echeverría wrote *El Matadero (The Slaughterhouse)*, the first Argentine work of literature, in which the cruelty to the cattle is a metaphor for the barbarous cruelty inflicted on men in the country. Although the slaughterhouse is no longer behind the arcades and has been scattered among dozens of meat processing plants outside the city limits, the rites of the sacrifice haven't changed. They've only added another step to the dance, the prod, consisting of two copper poles through which an electrical charge is generated. When it is applied to the animal's flank, the prod herds them towards the sacrificial ramps. In 1932, a police commissioner named Leopoldo Lugones, son of the great national poet – his namesake – realized the instrument could be useful in torturing human beings, and ordered tests of electrical charges on political prisoners, choosing soft areas where the pain would be most intolerable: the genitals, the gums, the anus, the nipples, the ears, the nasal cavities, with the intention of annihilating all thought or desire and converting the victims into non-persons.

I made a list of those details in the hope of finding a clue as to what had led Martel to sing in front of the old slaughterhouse, but although I went over it time and time again, I couldn't see it. Alcira Villar would have given me the key, but I didn't know her then. She later told me that Martel tried to recapture the past just as it had been, without the disfigurations of memory. He knew the past remained intact somewhere, not in the shape of the present but of eternity: what was and still continues to be will be the same tomorrow, something like Plato's Primordial Idea or Bergson's crystals of time, although the singer had never heard of them.

According to Alcira, Martel's interest in the mirages of time began in Tita Merello's cinema, one June day, when they went to see two movies Carlos Gardel had filmed at the Paramount studios in Joinville, *Melodía de arrabal (Suburban Melody)* and *Luces de Buenos Aires (Lights of Buenos Aires)*. Martel had observed his idol with such intensity that he felt at certain moments – he said then – that he was him. Not even the terrible condition of the prints had disappointed him. In the solitude of the theater, he sang softly, in a duet with the voice on screen, two of the tangos, *Tomo y obligo (I'll have a Drink and so will You)* and *Silencio*. Alcira couldn't hear the slightest difference between one singer and the other. When Martel imitated Gardel, *he was Gardel*, she said. When he strove to be himself, he was better.

They went back to see the two films again the next day at the matinee and, on the way out, the singer decided to buy copies on video that they sold in a shop on Corrientes at the corner of Rodríguez Peña. For a week he did nothing but watch them over and over again on the television, sleeping now and then, eating something, and watching them again, Alcira told me. He'd pause them to look at the rural landscape, the cafés of the day, the greengrocers' shops, the clubs. Gardel, on the other hand, he listened to spell-bound, without pauses. When it was all over, he told me that the past of films was an artifice. The tones of the voices were conserved as clearly as in the recordings they re-touched in the studios, but the surroundings were painted cardboard and, even though what we saw was the very same cardboard as the day it was filmed, the gaze degraded it, as if time contained a force of incorrigible gravity. Not even then did he stop thinking, Alcira told me, that the past was intact somewhere, maybe not in people's memories, as we might suppose, but rather outside of us, in some uncertain point in reality.

I didn't know any of this when I went to the arcades of the Liniers market at eleven-thirty the next morning, the day after my encounter with Valeria. Among a sea of cables, beside two trucks loaded with spotlights and sound systems, I made out the two young actors from La Brigada in patent leather high-heeled shoes. The filming had finished and I didn't approach them. The place was lit by the soft November sunlight and, despite the cracks of humidity and age, it still had a severe beauty. Behind the arcades were glimpses of entrance halls and stairways to the offices of a union, a pottery class and the neighborhood committee, while across the street was a sign for a Creole Museum I didn't care to visit. In the center, a sixty-foot-high tower topped with a clock threw its shadow across the Plazoleta del Resero, where a few tipas trees grew, like in Parque Lezama.

Although the street's hustle and bustle was incessant at this time of day as heaving buses went past, leaving a wake of asthmatic sounds, the air smelled of cows, calves and wet grass. While I waited for noon, I went into the market. An intricate web of corridors surrounded the corrals. Despite the late hour, two thousand head of cattle were waiting to be auctioned. The consignees executed an inimitable minuet in those galleries, one step of which was discussing the livestock prices among themselves, at the same time as writing hieroglyphics in their electronic appointment books, talking on their cell phones and exchanging signals with their colleagues, without getting confused or missing a beat. On one occasion I heard the cathedral-like bell ringing in the distance announcing the auction, while the drivers moved the cattle from one corral to another. After having seen *Faena*, knowing the fate that awaited each one of these animals – an inevitable fate that, nevertheless, had not yet happened – filled me with an unbearable despair. They're already in death's grip, I said to myself, but death will arrive tomorrow. What difference was there for them between the non-being of the present and the non-being of the next day? What difference is there now between what I am now and what this city will make of me: something that is happening to me right now and that, like the cows about to be sacrificed, I cannot see? What will Martel make of me while making something else of himself?

It would soon be midday and I sped up to arrive in time at the arcades. If the singer had reserved the whole place all to himself, maybe he would be accompanied by an orchestra. The thundering of trucks and buses would drown out his voice, but I would be right there to hear it. I would drink it if necessary. He could only get around in a wheelchair by then and couldn't stay in the same place for more than an hour: he was having convulsions and fainting fits, couldn't control his sphincter.

At quarter to one, however, he had still not arrived. The aroma of stews being cooked in the neighborhood converged on the Plazoleta de Resero and made me hungry. I hadn't slept and all night I'd had nothing but a couple of coffees in the Británico. From the beveled doorway of the Oviedo bar office workers and housewives emerged with packages of food, and I was tempted to cross the street and buy a bite to eat myself. I felt a bit light-headed and would have paid all the money I had for a plate of any old stew, though I didn't know if I'd really be able to enjoy it. I was worried, with an inexplicable anxiety, and had a vague premonition that Martel wasn't coming.

I never saw him arrive, in fact. I left the arcades about two-thirty. I wanted to be far away from the market, far from Mataderos and far from the world as well. A bus dropped me off a couple of blocks from the boarding house, beside a cheap restaurant where they served me a disgusting bowl of noodle soup. I got to my room just before five, hurled myself into bed and slept straight through till the next day.

When he alluded to a place, Martel was never literal, but each time I deceived myself thinking he was. If the little actors from La Brigada had told me he was going to evoke the Zwi Migdal's white slaves, I would have looked for him in any one of the brothels that association of pimps had operated around Junín and Tucumán Streets, in that block now purified by bookstores, video stores and film distributors. It wouldn't have occurred to me, for example, to go to the corner of Libertador and Billinghurst, where at the beginning of the last century there was a clandestine café, with a platform at the back, where women who'd been brought like cattle from Poland and France were auctioned off to the highest bidder. And I would much less have imagined that Martel might sing in the big house on Avenida de los Corrales where in 1977 the ex-prostitute Violeta Miller sent her nurse Catalina Godel to her death.

I waited in the Plazoleta del Resero and didn't see him, because he was inside a car that was stopped by the south corner of the arcades, with the guitarist Tulio Sabadell.

Only at the end of January, when I was leaving Buenos Aires, did I learn what had happened. Alcira Villar told me then that the singer had vomited blood that morning. When she took his blood pressure she realized it was extremely low. She tried to convince him not to go out, but he insisted. He was pale, his joints ached and his stomach was swollen. When we got him into the car, I thought we'd never arrive, Alcira told me. Fifteen minutes later, however, he had recovered. Sometimes his illness hid away somewhere inside his body, like a frightened cat, and other times it came out and showed its fangs. Martel was taken by surprise too but he knew how to calm it down and even pretend it didn't exist.

That morning we were driving along the Ezeiza highway, Alcira continued, and, when we were getting to General Paz Avenue, the pains retreated as unexpectedly as they'd begun. He asked me to stop so we could buy a spray of camellias and told me that after watching Gardel's films he'd decided to sing a couple of tangos from the 1930s. Over the last couple of days he'd been practicing *Margarita Gauthier*, which his mother used to sing as she washed clothes. 'It was a reflex action for her,' Martel had told her. 'She'd scrub the shirts and the tango would settle into her body of its own accord.' But that morning he wanted to start the private recital with *Volver* (*Return*), by Gardel and Le Pera.

Sabadell and I were surprised, Alcira told me, when he burst out singing in the car, in a baritone voice, a verse from *Return* that reflected, or at least to me seemed to reflect, his conflict with time: *I'm afraid of the showdown / with the past that returns / of confronting my life.* Stranger still was that he repeated the melody in F, in a deep bass voice and then, almost without a breath, he sang it as a tenor. I'd never heard him switch his voice from one register to another, because Martel was a natural tenor, and he never played with his voice this way again, at least not in front of me. He was very alert to our reactions, especially Sabadell's, who was staring at him incredulously. I only recall my admiration, because the transition from one to the other, far from jarring, was almost imperceptible, and even now I don't know how he did it.

Even before we got to the Avenida de los Corrales, Alcira told me, Martel went into one of his dark moods that worried me so much, and was completely silent, staring off into space. As we passed a house with balconies, which looked uninhabited, the only embellishment being a glass roof now in ruins, the driver of our car tried to park, perhaps obeying an order that Sabadell and I didn't know about. Only then did Martel emerge from his apparent apathy and ask him to continue on as far as the Plazoleta del Resero.

We didn't get out of the car, said Alcira. Martel asked Sabadell to lay the bunch of camellias at the entrance to a clinic, in the southern arcade, and to guard it for a moment so no one would take it. While he did that, the singer sat still with his head lowered, without saying a single word. Trucks pulling trailers, buses and motorcycles streamed past us but Martel's will for silence was so deep and dominant that I don't remember hearing anything, and what has remained are just the fleeting shadows of the vehicles, and the image of Sabadell, who looked naked without his guitar.

Two months later, during one of our long conversations in the Café La Paz, Alcira told me who Violeta Miller was and why Martel had left the camellias in the place where Catalina Godel was murdered.

I doubt you've heard of the Zwi Migdal, she said then. At the beginning of the twentieth century, almost all the brothels of Buenos Aires were run by that mafia of Jewish pimps. The Migdal's envoys traveled through the poorest villages of Poland, Galicia, Besarabia and the Ukraine, in search of Jewish girls they would seduce with false promises of matrimony. In some cases these illusory weddings would even take place in a synagogue where everything was faked: the Rabbi and the ten obligatory participants of the *minyan*. After a brutal initiation, the victims were confined in brothels where they worked fourteen to sixteen hours a day, until their bodies were reduced to ruins.

Violeta Miller was one of these women, Alcira told me. Third daughter of a tailor in the suburbs of Lodz, illiterate and without a dowry, one morning in 1914, she accepted, on the way out of synagogue, the company of a business-man with fine manners who paid her two more visits and on the third proposed. What the girl thought was the happiest moment of her life was actually the beginning of her downfall. On the ship, as she began her newlywed voyage to Buenos Aires, she found out that her husband had another seven wives on board, and that they were all destined for the whorehouses of Argentina.

The very night they arrived, she was auctioned in a lot with six other Polish girls. Wearing a school uniform, she stepped up onto the platform in the Café Parisién. Someone ordered her to hold up her hands and count on her fingers up to twelve if they asked her in Yiddish how old she was. In fact she was already fifteen, but she had very little body hair, no breasts and had only menstruated a few times, at irregular intervals.

The pimp who bought her ran a brothel with twelve young girls. He relieved Violeta of her virginity as a matter of course and, at dawn, when he heard her whimpering, whipped her into silence. The marks took a week to heal over. Thus, tormented and abused, she was obliged to serve from four the next afternoon until the following dawn, satiating dock workers and clerks who spoke to her in unintelligible tongues. She tried to escape, and they caught her a few meters from the house. The pimp punished her by branding her back with a cattle iron. To suffer all pains at once would be better than this purgatory, Violeta said to herself, and decided to fast to death. She lasted a week on nothing but one glass of water, and she would have let herself die if the madams who looked after her hadn't brought her a cardboard box with the ear of another fugitive inmate, warning her that, if she didn't give in, they'd leave her without eyes so she couldn't defend herself.

For five years, Violeta was moved from one whorehouse to another. She lived in Buenos Aires without knowing what the city was like: an electric light was always lit in her room so she couldn't distinguish between night and day.

The small size of her body attracted innumerable perverts, who thought she was prepubescent and mistook her lack of enthusiasm for inexperience. At the end of the summer of 1920 she contracted a tenacious fever that kept her laid up for months. She might have died if a bricklayer, who was also Polish, to whom Violeta had confided the story of her misfortunes, hadn't taken advantage of his visits to smuggle her in little bottles of glucose and antipyretic capsules. Two months later, when the poor thing was still convalescent, one of her companions in misery whispered that they were going to put her up for sale again. It was an atrocious piece of news, because her body was in a bad way from the fevers and so much use, and in the northern province of El Chaco, where unfortunates like her ended their days, girls were worked until their sphincters ruptured.

During the five and a half years of her martyrdom, Violeta had managed to save, centavo by centavo, the money from her tips. She had two hundred and fifty pesos, a fifth of what they'd paid for her at the first auction, and, now that she was worth nothing, it might have perhaps been enough to buy herself. That was impossible, because the women were only handed over to other men in the same business. Desperate, she asked the bricklayer if any-one he knew would be willing to pose as a pimp. It would have to be somebody bold. After many inquiries, a circus actor finally accepted the role. He introduced himself as an Italian, mentioned an imaginary brothel on the Isla Grande de Chiloé, and closed the deal in less than half an hour. A week later, Violeta was free.

She traveled in goods trains up to the northeast of Argentina. She stayed in some tedious town for a few months, working as a maid or in shops and, when she thought they'd discovered her trail, she fled to another town. Along the way she learned the alphabet and the Catholic catechism. At the end of the third winter she disembarked in Catamarca. There she felt safe and decided to stay. She took a room in the best hotel in the city and in a couple of weeks had spent almost all her savings. It was enough, because in that time she'd seduced the manager of the hotel and the treasurer of the provincial bank. Both were God and wife fearing, and Violeta got from them more than they could afford to give: one paid for her room for as long as she wanted to stay, the other got her a couple of low interest loans, and introduced her to the ladies of the Ministry of Prayer, who met on Fridays to say their rosaries. Determined to recover the happiness and respect she'd lost in her life of forced prostitution by any means necessary, Violeta opened her heart to them. She told them she'd been born Jewish, but that her greatest desire, since she was a little girl, was to receive the light of Christ. The ladies convinced the bishop to baptize her, and acted as her sponsors at the ceremony.

The city of Catamarca was devoted to the Virgin of the Valley, and Violeta took advantage of her connections to open a business dealing in religious objects, selling med-allions blessed in Rome, images of the Virgin for schools, votive offerings for the miraculously cured infirm and plenary indulgences for the dying. The pilgrims came from far and wide, and this steady stream made her a very rich woman. She was generous to the Church, supported a soup kitchen and the first Friday of every month took toys to the Children's Hospital. Her petite frame, which had caused her such grief in the brothels, was taken as a sign of refinement in Catamarca. Several men proposed to her, and Violeta turned each of her admirers down gently. I'm promised to Our Lord, she said to them, and I've offered him my chastity. This was at least half true: she had never been interested in sex, much less after all she'd had to endure by force. She hated the bitter sweat and violence of males. She hated the human race. At times she hated herself as well.

She lived like that for more than forty-five years. With inexpressible joy she read that the Zwi Migdal mafiosos had been caught one after the other thanks to the evidence of one brave victim, and she sent medallions of the Virgin to the commissioner and judge who put them in prison.

She never heard a word from her sisters, whom she imagined murdered in some concentration camp. She never wanted to return to Lodz, and even refused to watch the few films about the Holocaust shown in Catamarca. The only place she felt a melancholy nostalgia for was the Buenos Aires she was never allowed to know.

When she turned seventy, she decided to die as a lady in the city where she'd been nothing but a slave. On one of her rare visits to the capital, she bought a piece of land in the neighborhood of Mataderos, on the Avenida de los Corrales. She commissioned a renowned firm of architects to build a house identical to those she'd envied as a child in

Lodz, with a dining room to seat fourteen guests, a bedroom with wall to wall walk-in closets, marble bathtubs big enough to stretch out in, and a library with shelves up to the ceiling, packed with leather-bound volumes chosen by color and size. When the house was ready, she moved to Buenos Aires without saying goodbye to anyone.

Since she'd become fond of observing the constellations during her walks through the valleys of Catamarca, she stipulated that all the bedrooms of the new house should have roofs of reinforced glass, which obliged the architects to design an irregular angled structure with a complicated drainage system and very delicate waterproof covering, plus electrical mechanisms to open parts of the roof on clear days and close out the light of dawn.

The greatest luxury was, however, a raised marble platform to the right of the dining room, beside the parlor, enclosed by carved balusters, on top of which she had them mount an astronomical telescope and an armchair that fit her tiny body like a glove. The platform was reached by a cage-style elevator, operated by machinery that stuck out from the ceiling, hidden within a Tudor arch that was painted green.

In Buenos Aires she returned to the religion of her ancestors. She attended synagogue on Friday afternoons, learned to read Hebrew and had a *ketubah* written in the most elegant calligraphy certifying her false marriage of half a century ago. She mounted it in a bronze frame with symbols of the four seasons in relief and hung it in the most conspicuous place in the dining room. She had a gold mezuzah affixed to each of the doorposts in the house, with the name of the Almighty and verses from Deuteronomy.

Solitude, however, gave her sleepless nights. Alcira told me that two women took turns cleaning the house, but both of them had stolen lengths of silk and tried to break into her jewelry case. In 1975 shots were heard in the streets almost every night, and on television they talked of guerrilla attacks on barracks. She felt relieved when she knew the military had taken charge of the government and were rounding up everyone who opposed them. Her calm didn't last. In the late autumn of 1978 she had two falls when getting out of the bath as well as a number of severe asthma attacks. The doctor demanded she dispense with her mistrust and hire a nurse.

She interviewed fifteen applicants for the post, none of whom she liked. Some because they ate too quickly, others for treating her like an imbecilic child, others for expecting two days off a week. The last, who arrived when she'd given up hope, went even beyond what she'd imagined: she was diligent, quiet, and seemed so anxious to serve that she preferred – she said – only to leave the house when absolutely necessary: once every two weeks to do the shopping. Her letters of recommendation could not have been better, one written by a naval lieutenant who expressed his 'gratitude and admiration for the bearer, who cared devotedly for my mother for four years, until her demise,' and the other by a lieutenant commander who credited her with his wife's recovery.

Margarita Langman also had the advantage of her faith:

she was Jewish and God-fearing. Violeta began to depend on her like a parasite. No one had ever anticipated her desires. Margarita foresaw them even before she'd conceived them. Almost every night, while the elderly lady observed the constellations, the woman stood by her side, adjusting the telescope lenses and explaining the imperceptible rotations of Centaurus beneath the Southern Cross. She seemed immune to tedium. If she wasn't with Violeta, she was putting her suitcase in order or sewing. The television and radio transmitted nonstop government warnings, which accentuated the mistrust they both felt toward strangers. 'Do you know where your son is right now?' 'Do you know who's knocking at your door?' 'Are you sure you don't have an enemy of the fatherland sitting at your dining table?' Violeta was astute and thought herself able to identify deceitfulness in a person at first glance. Although she felt an instinctive trust towards Margarita, it seemed strange that she wouldn't give straight answers to questions about her family, and that neither of her brothers, of the two she said she had, ever visited her or called her on the phone. She was afraid she might not be what she seemed. Now that she'd known the pleasure of real company, she couldn't imagine her life without her.

One morning, when the nurse went out to the market for the fortnightly shopping, Violeta decided to snoop around in her room. Surreptitiously looking through the bags of other of the Migdal's prostitutes or her employees at the devotional shop in Catamarca had allowed her to save herself in time from robberies and slander. But this time, a few minutes after she'd crossed the threshold and when she'd barely had time to look at the neat bed with its embroidered pillow slips, a few books on the nightstand and the suitcase on top of the wardrobe, she heard noises at the front door and had to leave. Now she regretted having given Margarita a set of keys, but what could she do? The doctor had said another fall could leave her confined to bed and, in that case, she would be at the mercy of her guardian. It would be better to put her to the test before that happened.

I forgot my shawl, the nurse said. And besides, there were so many people in the market. I better go this afternoon instead. I don't like to leave you alone for so long.

Violeta spent the following week irritated even by hearing her washing the dishes. She paid her one hundred thousand pesos a month, and each centavo reminded her of her adolescent martyrdom. She hated the energy Margarita had even very late at night, when she'd been left with a plundered and pained body. She hated seeing her read, because she had never been allowed to have a book in her hands until she'd gotten free, at the age of twenty, when she no longer felt curiosity for any of them. She didn't like the way she looked at her, the shape of her head, her cracked hands, the monotony of her voice. But what incensed her most was never being alone in the house to go through her secret things.

For a long time, Alcira told me, the old lady had wanted to buy a diamond-studded gold Magen David. The need to put Margarita to the test finally made up her mind. All

Jewish girls dream of having one, and when she saw her piece of jewelry, she'd be envious. Did Violeta not know the human heart better than anyone? She impatiently summoned a goldsmith from Libertad Street and negotiated, millimeter by millimeter, the design and cost of a heavy 24 carat gold star with blue-toned diamonds in each of the six points, that would hang on a thick-linked chain.

One December morning, the jeweler announced that the Magen David was ready and offered to deliver it, but the old lady turned him down. She would rather, she said, have Margarita pick it up. It was her opportunity to get her away from the house for two or three hours. They argued bitterly about the matter. The nurse insisted that it wasn't prudent to abandon Violeta for such a long time, while she invented excuses to make her go.

Summer was near and it was extremely hot. Through the balcony shutters, Violeta spied on the nurse as she walked down Avenida de los Corrales toward the number 155 bus stop. She saw her cover her head with a scarf that hid half her face and take shelter in the shade of a tree. The air above the paving stones shimmered with heat. A bus came along. Once certain that Margarita had boarded, Violeta waited ten minutes and then triumphantly entered the forbidden room.

She didn't even leaf through the books on the nightstand. None of them looked important. A few dresses hung from coat hangers, arranged by color, two pairs of pants and two blouses. If Margarita was hiding something, it had to be in her suitcase, which she'd left on top of the wardrobe, out of reach. How to get it down? She discarded one method after another. Finally, she remembered the wheeled ladder the architects had sold her against their will.

She hadn't learned how to read in the whorehouses, but she'd picked up other skills: suspicion, robbery, lock picking. She was surprised by the ease with which, from the fourth step, leaning on the wardrobe, she managed to open the lock on the case and raise the lid. Disillusioned, she saw only a few poor quality shirts and a photo album.

On the first pages of the album were trivial family images, Alcira told me. Someone who must have been Margarita's father, with his shoulders covered by a *tallit*, hugged a little girl of ten or eleven, with an orphaned look in her eyes, defenseless against the hostility of the world. In other pictures, Margarita herself, dressed in a schoolgirl's smock, dodged the camera, was surprised blowing out a birthday candle, played in the sea. In the last one, with a windmill in the background, she smiled beside a man who could be her brother, although his skin was dark and his features looked Indian, like the peasants in northern Argentina. She had a baby just a few months old in her arms.

Hours later, when Violeta was being interrogated in the Stella Maris Church, she would say that, observing this last photo, she'd sensed her nurse's double life. A chill ran up my spine, she said in her statement. I thought the man in the picture was perhaps her husband, the baby her child. I realized I was entering into her past and now I couldn't leave it. At the edge, on one side of the photos I found a notebook I'd seen her with many times. It wasn't a diary, as

I'd often thought, but rather pages of meaningless sentences, dirty clippings of papers that said: *cheese, casserole, rude, I want, I love my mummy, my name is Catalina, my teacher's name is Catalina*, and at the end of each phrase a notation in a steadier hand: *Fermín, ask why they didn't give you a glass of milk – Tota, is Daddy or Mummy active in the M? Both? Repeat the 5 times table tomorrow.* Pages and pages of the same. Nothing caught my attention, Violeta would say to the officer who interrogated her. I was about to close the case and when I touched the lid I felt it was full of papers, objects, I don't know what, I was curious and scrupulous as well, because the papers were loose and the woman would know if I got them out of order. My hunches are infallible, however, and something in my heart told me she was guilty. I gathered up my courage, found the false bottom of the lid and pulled out some blank papers. All of them were stamped with embossed military letterhead and coats of arms, with the names of this admiral or that naval lieutenant. Further down I found unknown people's identity cards and civic passbooks. Some of them, however, had the woman's photo, sometimes with her hair dyed, and with other names, Catalina Godel, Catalina Godel, I remember that one clearly, Sara Bruski, Alicia Malamud, and some gentile surnames as well, Gómez, Arellano, who knows how many more. How could I have imagined that Margarita had been a teacher in Bajo Flores and that she'd escaped from a military prison. One doesn't know who's who anymore in these confusing times.

She stepped down off the ladder and stopped to think.

The nurse's reference letters were undoubtedly forged, and she had been an idiot not to have verified them by phone. Perhaps what they said was false but all the rest was undoubtedly true: the coat of arms with anchors and the embossed names of the officers. She had no time to waste. Then, with the sangfroid she'd learned from her years of slavery, she dialed the telephone number at the bottom of the letterhead. The officer on duty answered the phone. 'It's a matter of life or death,' she said, according to what Alcira told me later in the Café La Paz. The operator asked what number she was calling from and ordered her to stay on the line. Less than two minutes later the lieutenant commander was on the line. 'How fortunate it's you, sir,' Violeta said. 'Is the nurse I hired not the same one who took care of your wife?' 'Tell me the name that woman gave you. Name or names, the officer demanded. He had a rough, impatient voice, like the pimp who'd bought her in the Café Parisién. 'Margarita Langman,' said Violeta. Suddenly, she too felt hunted. The interminable past came crashing down on her. 'Describe her,' the captain pressed. The old lady didn't know how to do so. She spoke of the photo with the baby and the man with Andean features. Then, she gave her address on the Avenida de los Corrales, told him discreetly that she was seventy-nine years of age. 'That woman is a very dangerous character,' the officer said. 'We're on our way over there right now. If she gets there before we do, keep her there, distract her. You'd better not let her get away, eh? You'd better not let her get away.'

I, Bruno Cadogan, knew then that the camellias Sabadell

left in the Plazoleta del Resero weren't to commemorate the barbarous butchers of Echeverría's story and the film *Faena*, but some more recent, more ruthless ones. Alcira Villar said in the Café La Paz that, if they'd only stayed a few minutes in that corner of death, it was because Martel wanted to honor Catalina Godel not at the final point of her misfortunes but at the house where she'd hidden for almost six months, after having escaped from the Escuela de Mecánica de la Armada. What I don't understand, I said to Alcira, is why Martel reserved the arcades for a recital that he never gave. If you'd known him, she answered, you would have realized that he was no longer singing in public by then. He didn't like to be seen so haggard and weak. He didn't want to be bothered by anyone and while Sabadell was placing the bouquet of flowers he recited a tango under his breath for Catalina Godel. Maybe he'd initially intended to get out of the car and walk over to the clinic, I don't know for sure. Martel's plans were as hard to fathom as those of a cat.

FOUR

Catalina Godel left home at the age of nineteen, when she fell madly in love with a rural school teacher who was passing through Buenos Aires. Her mother's weeping, her father's lectures on the unhappiness she could expect from a man of another religion and lower social class, her older brothers' curses were all to no avail. She went to work at her lover's remote school in the deserts of Santiago del Estero. There she found out that he was a militant in the Peronist resistance and unhesitatingly embraced the same cause. After a few months she'd learned how to make Molotov cocktails quickly and became skilled at cleaning weapons and shooting targets. She discovered she was brave, ready for anything.

Although her companion sometimes disappeared for weeks at a time, Catalina didn't worry. She got used to not asking, to dissembling and to talking only when strictly necessary. The silence only weighed on her on New Year's Eve 1973, when she stayed alone in the little school, besieged by a dust storm while the earth seemed to burn beneath her feet. She heard on the radio, days later, that her companion had been taken prisoner while attempting to capture a traffic police post on General Paz Avenue, in Buenos Aires. She thought the action foolish and rash, but understood that the people were fed up with the abuses and it was necessary to act however possible. She packed her few items of clothing, her childhood photos, and a book by John William Cooke, *Peronism and Revolution*, which she knew by heart, in a canvas suitcase. She walked to the nearest village and from there took the first bus to Buenos Aires.

You can't imagine how much effort Martel and I put into finding out every detail of that life, Alcira Villar told me in the Café La Paz twenty-nine years later, just before I was to return to New York forever.

I used to see her as the evening began, around seven. For two months I'd been living in an airless little hotel, near Congreso. The heat and flies kept me from sleeping. As I walked towards the café, the asphalt melted beneath my feet. Although the air conditioning kept the La Paz at an even seventy-five degrees, the heat and humidity took hours to peel off me. More than once I stayed there, taking notes for this story, until the waiters began to pile up the tables and wash the floor. Alcira, on the other hand, always arrived looking radiant, and only occasionally, as the night wore on, would she get bags under her eyes. If I pointed this out, she'd touch them with the tips of her fingers and say, without any sarcasm: It's the happiness of getting old. She told me that she and the singer had discovered the story of Catalina while reading the minutes of the trials of the commanding officers under the dictatorship, and, although it wasn't much different from thousands of others, Martel was bewitched and for months could think of nothing else. He insisted on searching for witnesses who'd known Catalina on the Avenida de los Corrales or during her years of activism. A minor anecdote would lead to another, Alcira said, and gradually Violeta Miller's past emerged onto the scene. One of her Polish nephews traveled to Buenos Aires in 1993 to dispute the ownership of the big empty house. We learned how it had all started in Lodz from the nephew.

It took us almost a year to put together the pieces of the puzzle, Alcira continued. The two women had similar biographies. Catalina and Violeta had both been Jewish women subjected to servitude, and each of them, in their way, had defied their masters. Martel thought that, if they'd trusted each other more, told each other who they were and all that they'd suffered, maybe nothing would have happened to them. But they were both used to suspicion, and so, once separated, Violeta was overcome by fear and meanness and only Catalina could defend her dignity until the end.

After the attack on the traffic police post, Alcira told me, Catalina's lover was tried and locked up in the Rawson prison in Patagonia. He was released in May of 1973, but a year and a half later he had gone underground again. Perón had died leaving the government in the hands of his idiot wife and her astrologer who accumulated power by murdering enemies imaginary and real. At that time, Catalina decided to forge a fake ID for herself, that of Margarita Langman, and began to work as a teacher in Bajo Flores, where they let her use a small apartment without a bathroom. She was pregnant by then, and for a few days she considered returning to her parents' house, to be taken care of and to allow her baby to grow up in a happy domestic environment. That bourgeois weakness later struck her as a bad sign.

Her son was born in the middle of December, 1975. Although the father had been advised of the delivery by phone by Catalina herself – who was admitted to hospital under the name of Margarita – he didn't appear until a week later. Apparently, when the baby was born his father was submerged beneath the waters of the Río de la Plata, placing underwater mines on the *Itatí* yacht, property of the Naval High Command. The new family spent January and February hiding out in the house of a foreman of a ranch in Colonia, Uruguay, while they were searched for everywhere and Isabel Perón's government was falling to pieces. In that brief summer in Colonia, Margarita experienced a lifetime's worth of happiness. She and her companion took photographs, watched the sunset from the river's edge and walked hand in hand through the winding streets of the old city, pushing the baby carriage. They returned to Buenos Aires when the military, who had now struck their lethal blow, were murdering everyone they identified as subversives. The former school teacher was one of the first to fall, in April 1976. As soon as she found out, she left the baby in his grandmother's care and returned to Bajo Flores. She only left there to participate as a volunteer in the suicidal attacks the Montoneros carried out that year.

She was caught in a trap fourteen months later in the bar
Oviedo, in Mataderos, where she'd arranged another of her
clandestine meetings. As she walked in, she realized that the
place was surrounded by plainclothes military police. She
ran toward the arcades, tried to get on a bus as it was pulling
away. They cornered her, however, in the entranceway
where the clinic is now and took her, blindfolded, to a cellar
where they tortured and raped her, while they questioned
her about her sexual activity and people she barely knew.
After many hours – she never knew how many – they left
the ruins of her body in a place called Capucha, where other
prisoners survived with sacks over their heads. There she
began to heal as much as possible, drinking tiny sips of the
water they gave her and repeating her *nom de guerre* in the
darkness, Margarita Langman, I am Margarita Langman.
Months went by. She learned through the prisoners'
stealthy gossip that by pretending to break and gaining
the torturers' confidence, perhaps it might be possible to
escape and tell what had happened to them. She wrote a
confession renouncing her ideals, she handed it to a lieutenant and, when he suggested she read it before a television
camera, did so without flinching. She thus managed to be
sent to work in a forgery laboratory, where they created
false ownership papers for stolen cars, passports and visas
from foreign consulates. She gradually and patiently famil-
iarized herself with the names and ranks of her captors and
accumulated papers with official letterheads. She even
reached the point of falsifying documents for herself, some
of which featured her real name. She always carried these

documents with her in an envelope for photographic plates that no one would open for fear of exposing the contents.

She'd been working in the laboratory for a while when they ordered her to point out militants prowling around the neighborhood of Mataderos. It was to be the decisive proof of her loyalty, maybe the step before being set free. She went out with a patrol at seven in the evening. She sat in the passenger seat of a Ford Falcon, with three non-commissioned officers in the back. It was winter and a cold rain was falling. Arriving at the corner of Lisandro de la Torre and Tandil, a bus crashed into the side of the Ford and overturned it. The men traveling with Margarita were knocked out. She was able to escape through a window, with slight cuts on her arms and legs. Her biggest problem was how to get rid of the well-meaning people trying to take her to hospital. She was finally able to slip away into the darkness and seek refuge in Bajo Flores, where the military had been devastatingly effective and almost none of her friends were left. The next morning, in the classified section of *Clarín*, she read Violeta Miller's ad for a nurse, forged the letters of recommendation and turned up at the house on Avenida de los Corrales.

You know the rest, Alcira told me. The afternoon she was going to die, Catalina Godel, Margarita, or whatever you choose to call her now, returned from the jeweler's with the Magen David, almost at the same time as Violeta finished talking to the torturers. The old lady clung to life with tenacious fury, as the phrase in our national anthem goes. She so feared being discovered that she inevitably gave herself away. She began to tremble. She said she had a chill, that her back hurt and she needed a cup of tea. Let's leave the pestering till later, Margarita answered with unusual disdain. I'm drenched in sweat and dying for a shower.

Violeta then committed two errors. She had the Magen David case in her hand and inexplicably didn't open it. Instead, she raised her eyes and her gaze met that of Margarita. She saw a flash of comprehension. It all happened in a second. The nurse walked past Violeta as if she no longer existed and reached the front door. She ran across the cobbled paving of the avenue, took cover in the arcade on the Plazoleta del Resero and there her executioners caught up with her, in the very place where she'd been captured the first time.

They sent a Ford Falcon to pick up Violeta Miller every morning to take her to the Stella Maris church, on the other side of the city. There the lieutenant commander interrogated her, Alcira told me, sometimes for five or six hours. He dug up her past and shamed her with her double religious conversion. The elderly lady lost her notion of time. Her chronic osteoporosis was aggravated and, when the interrogation sessions ended, she could barely move. She had to resign herself to hiring nurses who treated her with the same severity as the madams of the brothels. Nothing made her suffer more, however, than the disorder she discovered when she returned each afternoon to the house on the Avenida de los Corrales. The house had been turned into the private preserve of the lieutenant commander, who set about stripping the marble fixtures from the bathrooms, the table from the dining room, the balusters from the small observatory, the elevator, the telescope, the embroidered sheets, the television. Even the strongbox where she kept her jewelry and her bearer's bonds was ripped out of the wall. The only objects left intact were a Cortázar novel that Margarita had left half finished and the empty sewing basket in the kitchen. The glass roof was perforated one day in two central points in the library, and the rain began to fall mercilessly on the wrecked books.

Do you remember how Sabadell left the spray of camellias at the southern arcade at noon? Alcira asked me. It was the 20th of November, of course I remember, I answered. I was there, waiting for Martel, and didn't see him. I already told you we didn't get out of the car, she repeated. We stayed there watching Sabadell while he set down the flowers and people came and went indifferently through the Plazoleta del Resero. The singer had his head down, without saying a word. His will for silence was so deep and dominant that all I remember of that morning are the fleeting shadows of the vehicles, and the image of Sabadell, who looked naked without his guitar.

From there we set off for the big house on Avenida de los Corrales, Alcira continued. The property was still under litigation and was worth less than the rubble. The parquet floors had been stripped long ago, and you couldn't take a step without the glass from the roofs crunching under your shoes.

Martel, in his wheelchair, asked us to take him into the kitchen. Without hesitation he opened one of the larders, as if the house were familiar to him. He took out a piece of rusty tin with bits of thread stuck on it and a damp copy of *Hopscotch*, which fell apart as soon as he tried to leaf through it. With these remains in his hands, he sang. I thought he'd begin with *Volver*, as he'd told us in the car, but he preferred to start with *Margarita Gauthier*, a tango written by Julio Jorge Nelson, the Widow of Gardel. *Today, overcome, I invoke you, my divine Margarita,* he said, lifting up his torso slightly. He carried on like that, as if he might levitate. The lyrics are sickly sweet, but Martel turned the song into a funereal sonnet worthy of Quevedo. When his voice attacked the three sugariest verses of the tango, I noticed his face was bathed in tears: *Today, on bended knee by the tomb where your body rests, / I've paid the tribute that your soul sighed, / I've brought you the spray of now wilting camellias . . .* I put a hand on his shoulder to get him to stop, because he could damage his throat, but he finished the song gracefully, rested a few moments and asked Sabadell for a few chords of *Volver*. Sabadell accompanied him knowingly, without allowing the guitar to compete with the voice: his strumming was more like a extension of the voice's excess light.

I thought when he finished *Volver* we'd leave, but Martel brought his hands up to his chest in an almost theatrical gesture, unexpected in him, and repeated the first verse of *Margarita Gauthier* at least four times, always in the same register. As the repetition advanced, the words gradually filled with meaning, as if they were collecting up as they went past all the voices that had pronounced them in other times. I remembered, Alcira said, having a similar experience during certain films with a fixed image that stays on the screen for more than a minute: the image doesn't change, but the person watching it starts to become another. The act of seeing imperceptibly turns into the act of possessing. *Today, overcome, I invoke you, my divine Margarita*, sang Martel, and the words were no longer outside our bodies but flowing into our bloodstreams, can you understand that, Bruno Cadogan? Alcira asked me. I answered that a long time ago I'd studied a similar idea by the Scottish philosopher David Hume. I quoted: Repetition changes nothing in the object repeated, but in the spirit which contemplates it. That's what it was like, said Alcira. That phrase clearly defines what I felt. When I heard Martel sing *my divine Margarita* the first time that afternoon, I didn't think he was changing the tempo of the melody, but the second or third time I noticed that he was subtly spacing each word. It's possible he was also spacing the syllables, although my ear isn't sharp enough to tell. *Today, overcome, I invoke you*, he sang, and the Margarita of the tango returned to the big house, as if time had not passed, with her body of twenty-four years earlier. *Today, overcome, I invoke you*, he said, and I felt that this summons was enough to make the glass on the floor vanish and the cobwebs and dust fade away.

December 2001

My missed encounter with Martel in the Plazoleta del Resero disturbed me. I lost track of what I was writing and I lost track of myself. I spent several nights in the Británico observing the desolate landscape of the Parque Lezama. When I returned to the boarding house and managed to sleep, the slightest unexpected noise would wake me. I didn't know what to do about the insomnia and, in dismay, I went out walking through Buenos Aires. Sometimes I strayed off from the ruined Constitución Station, about which Borges had written so much, towards the neighborhoods of San Cristóbal and Balvanera. The streets all looked the same and, although the newspapers called attention to the constant attacks, I didn't feel in danger. Gangs of boys no more than ten years old roamed around Constitución. They came out of their shelters looking for food, protecting each other, and asking for spare change. You could see them sleeping in the hollow buildings, covering their faces with newspapers and bags of leftovers. Many people were sleeping rough and, where I saw two one night, I'd find three or four the next. From

Constitución I'd walk down San José or Virrey Cevallos to Avenida de Mayo, and then cross the Plaza de los Dos Congresos, with its benches occupied by destitute families. More than once I spent hours of wakefulness at the corner of Rincón and México, spying on Martel's house, but always in vain. Only once did I see him leave with Alcira Villar at midday – although I didn't know who she was until weeks later – and, when I tried to follow him in a taxi, a group of demonstrating pensioners blocked my way.

Even though the city was a flat grid, I couldn't manage to get my bearings, due to the monotony of the buildings. Nothing is more difficult than noticing the subtle changes in something unchanging, like in a desert or on the sea. Confusion sometimes paralyzed me on any given street corner and, when I emerged from the shock, it was to circle round in search of a café. Fortunately, there were cafés open at all hours, and I'd sit in them and wait until, with the first light of dawn, the houses recovered profiles that allowed me to recognize them. Only then would I return to the boarding house by taxi.

Insomnia weakened me. I had hallucinations in which photos of early twentieth-century Buenos Aires would superimpose themselves on images of reality. I would lean out the balcony of my room and, instead of the vulgar buildings across the street, I'd see the terrace of Gath & Chaves, a shop that had disappeared from Florida Street forty years ago, where gentlemen in straw hats and ladies in starched collars drank cups of hot chocolate before a horizon bristling with spires and empty balconies, some of them crowned with Hellenic statues. Or I'd see the absurd dolls that used to advertise analgesics and aperitifs in the 1920s. The unreal scenes went on for hours, and during this time I didn't know where I was, because the past installed itself in my body as strongly as the present.

I met El Tucumano almost every night in the Británico. We argued over and over again about the best way to get Bonorino out of the cellar without ever agreeing. Perhaps it wasn't a problem of means but of ends. For me, the aleph – if it existed – was a precious object that couldn't be shared. My friend, on the other hand, was intending to degrade it, turning it into a fairground attraction. We'd found out that, at the death of the Bulgarian aristocrat, the boarding house was sold to some investors in Acassuso, who owned another twenty rented houses. We decided that I should write them a letter denouncing the librarian, who hadn't paid any rent since 1970. It would be detrimental to the finance manager and perhaps also to poor Enriqueta. None of this bothered El Tucumano.

Towards the end of November, NYU sent me an unexpected remittance of money. El Tucumano suggested we forget the bohemian scrimping of boarding-house life and go spend a night in the suite on the top floor of the Hotel Plaza Francia, where we could look out over the Libertador Avenue and some of its palaces, as well as buoys of the north shore that twinkled above the unmoving waters of the river. Although it wasn't a first-class hotel, that room cost two hundred dollars, more than my resources would allow. I didn't want to say no, though, and I paid for a reservation for the following Friday in advance. We thought we'd have dinner first in one of the restaurants in Recoleta that served *signature cuisine*, but that day an unforeseen misfortune occurred: the government announced that people could only withdraw a minuscule percentage of cash from their accounts. I was afraid of being left with nothing in my pocket. From the very moment of the sudden decree – too late to cancel the hotel – no one wanted to accept credit cards and the value of money became vague.

We got to the Plaza Francia around midnight. The air was the color of fire, as if a storm were brewing, and the streetlights all seemed muffled in watery hoods. Every once in a while a car drove down the avenue, slowly, bewildered. I thought I saw a couple kissing at the foot of the statue of General Alvear, under our balcony, but everything was shadowy and I'm not sure of anything, not even the peace with which I took off my clothes and lay down in bed. El Tucumano stayed outside for a while, scanning the profile of the Río de la Plata. He came back into the room in a bad mood, bitten by mosquitos.

The humidity, he said.

The humidity, I repeated. Like in Kuala Lumpur. Less than a year before I had confused the two cities. Maybe, I told him, it was because I'd read a story about mosquitos that was set here in February 1977. An irritating stink of fish invaded Buenos Aires then. Millions of dorados, pejerreyes and catfish, poisoned by the factories the military protected, lay rotting on the drought-enlarged shores. The dictatorship had imposed an iron censorship and none of the newspapers dared publish anything about this, despite the fact that the inhabitants, through the unavoidable use of their senses, received constant confirmation. Since the water from the taps had a strange greenish color and looked infected, those who were not extremely poor emptied the stores of soda water and fruit juice. In the hospitals, where they expected an epidemic from one day to the next, they dispensed thousands of vaccinations against typhoid daily.

One afternoon, a cloud of mosquitos rose up from the swamps and blackened the sky. It happened all of a sudden, like a biblical plague. People got covered in welts. In the forty blocks north of the Cathedral, where the banks and bureaux de changes were clustered, the smell of the river was intolerable. Some rushed pedestrians who had to conduct some financial transactions covered their faces with white masks, but the police patrols forced them to remove them and show their identity documents. On Corrientes Street, people walked along with lit mosquito coils, despite the furious heat, bonfires were lit on some corners in an attempt to disperse the insects. The plague receded as suddenly as it had arrived. Only then did the newspapers publish, on inside pages, brief articles that all had a similar title: 'Inexplicable phenomenon.'

While we slept in the hotel, a fierce wind began to blow at about two in the morning. I had to get up to close the suite's windows. El Tucumano woke up then, and asked me who I was looking at from the balcony.

No one, I said. And I told him about the wind.

Don't lie, he answered me. You lie so much, I don't know if you've ever told the truth.

Come over here, look at the sky, I said. It's clear now. You can see the stars over the river.

You're always changing the subject, Bruno. What do I care about the sky? The only thing I care about is your lies. If you want the alé all for yourself, tell me. I've had enough. It's all the same to me now if I get stood up. But don't string me along, big guy.

I swore I didn't know what he was talking about, but he was still anxious, hyper, as if he'd taken an overdose. I knelt down beside him, next to the bed, and stroked his head, trying to calm him down. It was useless. He turned his back on me and switched out the light.

El Tucumano's moods were incomprehensible to me. We didn't have any commitment to each other and each one was free to do as he liked, but when I stayed up till dawn working in the Británico, he'd come and find me and make jealous scenes in public that embarrassed me. He asked me to do difficult things for him, or for gifts, to put me to the test, and as soon as I began to satisfy his desires, he'd pull away. Not really knowing what he expected of me was maybe what most attracted me.

Exhausted, I slept. Three hours later I woke up with a start. I was alone in the suite. On the table in the hall El Tucumano had left a note scribbled in pencil: 'I'm off, Titan. I leave the alé to you as an inheritance. One day you can pay me back.' I went over the events of the previous night to understand what could have bothered him and couldn't think of anything. I wanted to leave the hotel right then, but it was crazy to go downstairs and ask for the bill without any explanation. For half an hour or more I was sitting in the suite's little living room with my mind a blank, submerged in that state of despair that makes the simplest movements impossible. I didn't dare close my eyes for fear that reality might desert me. I saw how the grey glare of the morning advanced over me and how the air, which had seemed so humid the night before, thinned to transparency.

I stood up after an effort, feeling like someone had laid the body of a sick man across my shoulders, and went to the balcony to watch the sunrise. The globe of the sun, huge and invasive, rose above the avenue, and its golden tongues licked the parks and sumptuous buildings. I doubt there has ever existed a city as beautiful as Buenos Aires at that moment. The traffic was heavy unusual for so early on a Saturday morning. Hundreds of cars moved slowly along the avenue, while the light charged the bronze of the monuments and burned the crests of the towers before falling bloodlessly through the leaves of the trees. The cupola of the Palais de Glace, beneath my balcony, was suddenly split by a blazing sword. In some of its salons in the 1920s, and other decades – when it was known as Vogue's Club – they'd danced the tango to Julio de Caro's sextet and Osvaldo Fresedo's orchestra. As the sun rose and its disk became smaller and blinding, a purple light washed the façade of the Bellas Artes Museum, where I'd contemplated scenes of the Battle of Curupaytí that Cándido López had painted with his left hand between 1871 and

1902, after the right one was blown off in a grenade explosion.

I had the impression then that Buenos Aires was hanging weightless in that icy clarity, and I feared that, pulled by the sun's attraction, it would disappear from sight. All the bad omens of an hour earlier vanished. I didn't feel I had the right to unhappiness while watching how the city blazed within a circle that reflected others above it, like the ones Dante saw at the center of paradise.

Pure sensations tend to get mixed up with impure ideas. It was at that moment, I think, when, after deciding to write a letter to El Tucumano describing the spectacle he'd missed, I completed a different one, addressed to the Acassuso investors, in which I denounced the illegal occupation of the cellar, for more than thirty years, by the librarian Sesostris Bonorino. I don't know how to reconcile the ignoble lines my hand was writing with the thoughts of the dazzling light I'd just seen. I had wanted to say to my friend that, since we didn't come from Buenos Aires, he and I were perhaps more sensitive than natives to its beauty. The city had been raised at the limits of an unvarying plain, among scrubland as useless for nourishment as it was for basket-making, on the edge of a river whose single redeeming feature was its enormous width. Although Borges tried to ascribe it a past, the one it now has is also smooth, without any heroic feats other than those improvised by its poets and painters, and each time one took any fragment of the past in hand, it was only to watch it dissolve into a monotonous present. It's always been a city where the poor were plentiful and where one had to walk with occasional jumps to dodge piles of dog shit. Its only beauty is what the human imagination attributes to it. It's not surrounded by sea and hills, like Hong Kong and Nagasaki, nor does it lie on a trade route along which civilization has navigated for centuries, like London, Paris, Florence, Geneva, Prague and Vienna. No traveler arrives in Buenos Aires en route to somewhere else. Beyond the city there is no somewhere else: the spaces of nothing that open up to the south were called, on sixteenth-century maps, Land of Unknown Sea, Land of the Circle and Land of Giants, the allegorical names of non-existence. Only a city that had denied so much beauty can have, even in adversity, such an affecting beauty.

I left the hotel before eight in the morning. Since I had no desire to return to the boarding house, where the Saturday morning commotion was usually maddening, I took refuge in the Británico. The café was empty. The only waiter was sweeping up the overnight clients' cigarette butts. I took the letter to the Acassuso investors out of my pocket and reread it. It was overworked, malign and, though I had no intention of signing it, everything in it gave me away. It contained, in summary, the facts Bonorino had confided to me. Not for a single instant did I think of the damage I was doing to the librarian. I just wanted them to expel him from the cellar so I could comfortably find out if the aleph existed, as everything seemed to indicate. And so I could find out what would happen within me when I saw it.

Just before noon I returned to my room. I stayed there for a few hours trying to make some headway on my thesis, but

I couldn't concentrate. Worry eventually got the better of me and I went out to look for El Tucumano, who was still sleeping on the roof. I was hoping that when he saw the letter, he'd show gratitude, happiness, enthusiasm. None of that. He protested because I'd woken him up, read it indifferently, and told me to leave him alone.

For the next two days I wandered from one side of the city to the other with the same sadness I'd felt before dawn in the Hotel Plaza Francia. I walked through Villa Crespo trying to find Monte Egmont Street, where the protagonist of *Adán Buenosayres* lived. That was another novel I'd written an essay on when I did my MA, but none of the people in the neighborhood could tell me where it was. 'From Monte Egmont Street the aroma of paradises no longer rises,' I recited to them, in case the phrase might refresh their sense of direction. The only thing I achieved was to make them flee from me.

The following Friday at midday, as the heat intensified, I went into Chacarita cemetery. Some of the tombs were extravagant, with large glass doors that let you peer inside at the altar and coffins covered with lace mantles. Others were adorned with statues of children struck by lightning bolts, sailors peering through a spyglass at an imaginary horizon, and matrons ascending to heaven carrying their cats in their arms. The majority of the graves, however, consisted of a headstone and a cross. Turning down one of the avenues, I came across a statue of Aníbal Troilo playing the bandoneón with a pensive expression. Beyond it, Benito Quinquela Martín's raw colors adorned the columns that flanked his tomb, and even the painter's coffin was covered in loud arabesques. I saw bronze eagles flying over a bas-relief of the Andes, and the poet Alfonsina Storni entering a granite sea, while the Galvez brothers' hearses crashed next door. When I stopped before the monument to Agustín Magaldi, who'd been Evita Perón's boyfriend and was still strumming his guitar for eternity, I heard some heartrending laments in the distance and imagined they must be coming from a funeral. I walked towards the commotion. Three women in full mourning, with veils over their faces, were weeping at the foot of the statue of Carlos Gardel. They lit a cigarette for him and placed it between his greenish lips, while other women left floral crowns before the Madre María, whose talent for miracles improved with each passing year, according to the plaques on her tomb.

Around two in the afternoon I left by Elcano Avenue and walked north, with the hope of eventually arriving at a field or the river. The extension of the metropolis, however, was invincible. I remembered a J.G. Ballard short story, which imagined a world made entirely of cities joined by bridges, tunnels and almost imperceptible ocean currents, where humanity was suffocating as if it were in an anthill. Nothing in the streets I walked that day, however, reminded me of Ballard's colossal buildings. They were shaded by old trees, jacarandas and plane trees, which protected the neo-classical and colonial mansions, and the odd pretentious aviary. When I noticed I'd arrived at José Hernández Street, in the neighborhood of Belgrano, I imagined I must be near the plot of land where the author of *Martín Fierro* had lived out his last happy years, despite the critics' increasing contempt for the book – which, only thirty years after his death, in 1916, would be exalted by Leopoldo Lugones as the 'great national epic poem' – and the cruel battles to federalize the city of Buenos Aires, an idea he had championed. Hernández was a physically imposing man with such a powerful booming voice they called him 'Matraca' in the Chamber of Deputies. At the gargantuan banquets he offered at his country house, several hours' gallop from the city center, Hernández's guests admired his appetite as much as his erudition, which enabled him to quote complete texts of Roman, English and Jacobin laws that no one had ever heard of. He was tormented by 'fits,' as he called his attacks of gluttony, but he couldn't stop eating. A myocarditis laid him up in bed for five months, until he died one October morning, surrounded by an immediate family of more than one hundred, all of whom were able to hear his last words: 'Buenos Aires . . . Buenos Aires . . .'

In spite of walking the entire length of José Hernández Street, I didn't find a single reference to his place. I saw instead plaques paying homage to lesser heroes of the national literature, like Enrique Larreta and Manuel Mujica Láinez, on the fronts of mansions on Juramento and O'Higgins Streets. After a few turns I came out at the Barrancas of Belgrano, which in Hernández's time had been the city limits. There, the park designed by Charles Thays not long after the poet's death was now surrounded by imposing apartment buildings. A fountain decorated with valves and marble fishes, and a gazebo that might have been used for Sunday concerts, were all that was left of its rural past. The river had receded by more than a mile, and it was impossible to see it. In a painting of refined beauty, *Washer-women in Lower Belgrano*, Prilidiano Pueyrredón depicted the calmness usual in this area. Although the title of the oil painting alludes to women in plural, it shows only one, with a baby in her arms and a gigantic bundle of clothing balanced on her head, while an even bigger bundle is carried by a horse who comes along behind, riderless. On the gentle curve of the hills, then lonely and wild, two ombues with their cleaving roots, in open combat with the rough water of the river, the beaches of which are trodden by the washerwoman at this early morning hour. Buenos Aires then had a green color, almost golden, and no future sullied the desolation of its only hill.

When it started to get dark, I wearily went back to the boarding house. A cruel commotion awaited me. My neighbors were throwing mattresses, blankets and bundles of clothing down the stairs into the hallway. In the kitchen, Enriqueta was sobbing with her eyes fixed on the floor. From the cellar came the industrious rustling of Bonorino's index cards. I went over to Enriqueta, offered her tea and tried to console her. When I managed to get her to speak, I too felt like the world was ending. A poem by Pessoa buzzed through my mind over and over again; it began: *If you want to kill yourself, why don't you go ahead and kill yourself?* No matter how I much I swatted it away, it would not leave me alone.

At three o'clock that afternoon – Enriqueta told me –

two police officers and a notary had arrived at the house with orders to evict all the tenants. They demanded proof of payment and gave refunds to everyone who was up to date on their rent. As far as I understood, the owners had sold the building to a firm of architects, and they wanted to move in as soon as possible. When Bonorino read the judicial notification, which granted only twenty-four hours to vacate the premises, he stood motionless in the hallway in a state of absence that Enriqueta's screams couldn't break through until finally he held his hand to his chest, said. 'My God, my God,' and disappeared into the cellar.

Although the letter I'd sent to the investors in Acassuso had nothing to do with what was happening, I would still have liked to unwind the course of time. I found myself repeating another line of Pessoa's: '*God have mercy on me, who had none for anybody.*' When an author or a melody started going round in my head, it took ages to get rid of it. And Pessoa, of all people! Who, in the midst of such despair, could love a desperate poet? *Poor Bruno Cadogan, who matters to no one. Poor Bruno Cadogan, who feels so sorry for himself.*

Besides, my hands were tied. I couldn't help anyone. I'd idiotically spent two hundred dollars on a single night in the Hotel Plaza Francia and I couldn't get the tiny bit of money I had left out of the bank. And they might as well stop depositing my grant payments, because the banks were seizing all remittances. On Sunday I'd tried to recover a few pesos, standing in the enormously long lines in front of the automatic teller machines. Three of the machines ran out of cash before I'd advanced four feet. Another five were empty but people refused to admit it and kept punching in their requests, in the hope of some miracle.

Towards midnight, the neighbors from the next-door room told me jubilantly that they were going to take refuge in Fuerte Apache, where some relatives lived. When I told Enriqueta, she reacted as if to a tragedy.

Fuerte Apache, she said, separating the syllables. I wouldn't go for love nor money. I don't know how they can take those poor children there.

I was tormented by guilt and, nevertheless, I had nothing to feel guilty about. Or perhaps I did: after all, I had been malicious and cowardly enough to send that useless letter to the Acassuso misers accusing Bonorino, taking advantage of his confessions to me in the cellar. In Buenos Aires, where friendship is a cardinal and redeeming virtue, as can be deduced from tango lyrics, every informer is a bastard. There are at least six scornful words: snitch, stoolie, grass, nark, squealer, fink. I was sure El Tucumano considered me a despicable person. He'd asked me more than once to write the letter, thinking I'd cut off my hands before doing so. For someone like me, who believed that language and deeds were linked in a literal way, my friend's attitude was difficult to understand. Informing hadn't been easy for me either. However, the aleph had mattered more to me than the indignity.

I saw the gigantic woman who was washing a blouse in the bidet the afternoon I arrived again. She was going down the stairs with a mattress on her back, gracefully avoiding the obstacles. Her body was dissolving in sweat, but her makeup remained intact on her eyes and lips. Life sings the same for everyone, she said when she saw me, but I don't know if she was talking to me or herself. I was standing in the middle of the hallway, feeling like another piece of furniture on the set. At that moment I realized that sing could be another synonym for betray.

Bonorino's bald head peered out of the half-light of the stairway. I tried to get away, so I wouldn't have to look him in the face. But he'd come out of the cellar to talk to me.

Come down here, Cadon, please, he said. I was getting used to the mutations of my surname.

The index cards had disappeared from the stairway, and the gloomy dwelling, with its street-level windows barely letting in a miserly light, reminded me of the principal passage of the cave that Kafka described in 'The Burrow,' six months before he died. Just like the rodent of the story piling his provisions against one of the walls, taking pleasure in the diversity and intensity of the odors they emitted, Bonorino leaped around in front of the fruit crates that had served as his bedside tables and which now, stacked on top of five or six more, blocked off the minuscule bathroom and kitchenette. He was keeping the possessions he'd saved in them. I managed to make out the thesaurus, the shirts and the gas heater. The walls held the shadows of the papers that had been stuck on them for so many years, and the only piece of furniture that remained in place was the bedstead, although now stripped, with no sheets or pillows. Bonorino clutched to his chest the accounts ledger where he'd noted down the diverse information from the colored index cards. The ashen lamp with its twenty-five-watt bulb barely illuminated his hunchbacked body, upon which the world's ills seemed to have fallen.

Sad news, Cadon, he said. The light of knowledge has been condemned to the guillotine.

I'm sorry, I lied. You never know why these things happen.

Whereas I can see all that has been lost: the squaring of the circle, the domestication of time, the act of the first founding of Buenos Aires.

Nothing will be lost if you're well, Bonorino. May I pay for your hotel for a few days? Allow me this favor.

I've already accepted the invitation of other outcasts, who've offered me shelter in Fuerte Apache. You're a foreigner, there's no reason for you to take responsibility for anything. We serve our Lord in possible things and content ourselves with desiring the impossible ones, as Saint Theresa said.

I remembered how desperate Carlos Argentino Daneri was when they announced the demolition of the house on Garay Street, because if he was deprived of the aleph he would never be able to finish his ambitious poem called 'The Earth.' Bonorino, who had invested thirty years in the laborious entries of the National Encyclopedia, seemed indifferent. I didn't know how to ask tactfully about his treasure. I could allude to the polished space under the last step, to the sketch of the Stradivarius I'd glimpsed on my first visit. He himself provided the solution.

Count on me if there's anything I can do, I told him, hypocritically.

Indeed. I was going to ask you to look after this notebook, which is the distillation of my sleepless nights. You can give it back to me before you return to your country. I've heard that rats and robbers live side by side in Fuerte Apache. If I lose the cards, I lose nothing. They just contain drafts and copies of other imaginations. What I have truly created is in the notebook and I wouldn't know how to protect it.

You don't even know me, Bonorino. I could sell it, betray you. I could publish the work under my name.

You would never betray me, Cadon. I don't trust anyone else. I have no friends.

That candid declaration revealed the librarian could not have the aleph. He would only have had to look at it once to know that El Tucumano and I had betrayed him. Carlos Argentino Daneri hadn't been able to prevent the demolition of his house either, in Borges' short story. In the luminous point that reproduced Dante's Paradise, you couldn't see the future, therefore, you couldn't see reality either. The simultaneous and infinite facts it contained, the inconceivable universe, were only residues of the imagination.

I believed you at least had the aleph, I risked.

He looked at me and started to laugh. There were only five or six teeth left in his huge mouth.

Lie down under the nineteenth step right now and see for yourself if I have it, he said. I've spent hundreds of nights there, in a supine position, hoping to see it. Maybe in the past there was an aleph. Now it's vanished.

I felt dizzy, lost, loathsome. I took the ledger, which weighed almost as much as me, and I didn't want to take the volume on labyrinths I'd lent him.

Keep it as long as you want, I said. You're going to need it more than me in Fuerte Apache.

He didn't even thank me. He looked me up and down with a brazenness that contradicted his habitual unctuousness. What he did next was even more extravagant. He began to recite, with a rhythmic and well-modulated voice, a shantytown rap, while clapping his hands: *In the Fort there's no place to run / Life gets blown to kingdom come / If I live, it's where it smells like dung / If I die, it's a bullet from a stranger's gun.*

That's not bad at all, I said. I didn't know you had such talents.

I'm no Martel but I get by, he answered.

I'd never thought he might know Martel.

What? You like Martel?

Who doesn't? he said. Last Thursday I went to visit a colleague at the library in Parque Chas. Someone told us he was on a corner, singing. He arrived out of the blue and knocked out three tangos. We got to hear two. It was supreme.

Parque Chas, I repeated. I don't know where that is.

Right here, on the way into Villa Urquiza. Strange neighborhood, Cadon. The streets are circular and even the taxis get lost. It's a shame it doesn't appear in Prestel's book, because of the many labyrinths in the world, that's the biggest of all.

FIVE

December 2001

When they closed the boarding house on Garay Street I went to stay in a modest hotel on Callao Avenue, near Congreso. Although my room overlooked an interior patio, the traffic noise was enough to drive you crazy at any hour of the day or night. I tried to resume my work in the nearby cafés but people rushed in and out of them all complaining about the government at the tops of their voices. I preferred to return to the Británico where at least I knew the routine. There I found out from the waiter that El Tucumano was exhibiting his little mirrored aleph in the cellar of a union office, sharing the proceeds with the night watchman who let him in. Ten or twelve tourists attended the first show, but the second and third had to be canceled due to lack of interest. I supposed that, ignoring my advice, El Tucumano had omitted the reading of the fragment of Borges I'd pointed out to him: *I saw the teeming sea; I saw daybreak and nightfall; I saw the multitudes of America; I saw a silvery cobweb in the center of a black pyramid; I saw a tattered labyrinth (it was London).* Exposed without this text, the illusion the aleph created must have been precarious, and the tourists undoubtedly left disenchanted. To deceive even just ten tourists was a colossal success in those uneasy weeks. No one had any money in Buenos Aires (including me), and visitors fled the city as if the plague were approaching.

At dusk, when the traffic roared and my intelligence was defeated by the prose of the postcolonial theorists, I kept myself occupied by leafing through Bonorino's ledger, full of diligent illustrated definitions of words like dagger, twine, Uqbar, *maté*, fernet, percale, as well as including an extensive section on Argentine inventions such as the ballpoint pen, *dulce de leche*, fingerprinting and the electric cattle prod, two of which were due not to native ingenuity but to a Dalmatian and a Hungarian.

The references were inexhaustible and, if I opened the volume at random, I never encountered the same page, just like in *The Book of Sand*, which Bonorino quoted frequently. One evening I stumbled upon a long section about Parque Chas, and while I was reading it thought it was about time I went to see the neighborhood where Martel had most recently sung. According to the librarian, the spot owed its name to some infertile fields inherited by a Doctor Vicente Chas, in the center of which rose the smokestack of a brickworks. Shortly before his death in 1928, Doctor Chas brought a fierce lawsuit against the municipal government of Buenos Aires, which wanted to close down the furnace because of the damage it was causing to the lungs of the residents of the area, at the same time as it impeded the extension of the western route of the Avenida de los Incas, blocked by the beastly smokestack. The truth was that the municipality chose this place to implement an ambitious radial-centric project designed by the young engineers Frehner and Guerrico. The design copied the labyrinth, representing terrestrial sin and the hope of redemption, which lies beneath the cupola of the San Vitale church in Ravenna.

Bonorino speculated, however, that the circular layout of the neighborhood followed a secret communist and anarchist plan to provide themselves a refuge in times of uncertainty. His thesis was inspired by the passion for conspiracies that characterizes the inhabitants of Buenos Aires. How else to explain that the major diagonal street was called The Internationale before it became General Victoria Avenue, or that Berlín Street should figure on some maps as Bakunin, and that a short four-hundred-meter-long road was called Treveris, in allusion to Trier or Trèves, the birthplace of Karl Marx?

'A colleague from the Monserrat library, who lived in Parque Chas,' noted Bonorino in his book, 'guided me one morning through this tangle of zigzags and detours as far as the corner of Ávalos and Berlín. To put the difficulties of the labyrinth to the test, he insisted that I go one hundred meters in any direction and then return by the same route. If I took more than half an hour, he promised to come looking for me. I got lost, although I couldn't say whether it was on the way out or on the way back. *The intolerable white sun of high noon had already become the yellow sun which precedes nightfall*, and no matter how many turns I took, I could not manage to get my bearings. On an inspired impulse, my colleague tracked me down. It was getting dark when he finally saw me on the corner of Londres and Dublin, a few steps from where we'd parted. I seemed shaken and thirsty, he said. When I returned from the expedition, I developed a persistent fever. Hundreds of people have gotten lost in the deceptive streets of Parque Chas, where the interstice that divides the reality from the fictions of Buenos Aires would seem to be located. In every great city there is, of course, one of these lines of high density, similar to the black holes in space, which changes the nature of those who cross it. By reading old telephone books I deduced that the danger point is in the rectangle bordered by Hamburgo, Bauness, Gándara and Bucarelli Streets, where some of the houses were inhabited, seven decades ago, by Helene Jacoba Krig, Emma Zunz, Alina Reyes de Aráoz, María Mabel Sáenz and Jacinta Vélez, who were later turned into fictional characters. But the people of the neighborhood situate it on the Avenida de los Incas, where the ruins of the brickworks remain.'

What Bonorino said didn't help me to understand why Martel had sung in Parque Chas. The delirium about the dividing line between reality and fiction had nothing to do with his earlier attempts to capture the past – I never believed the singer was interested in the past of the imagination – and some of the popular stories about the adventures of the bandit Pibe Cabeza and other unsavory characters in the labyrinth had no links – if they were true – to the greater history of the city.

I spent two afternoons in the Congreso library to find out

about life in Parque Chas. I discovered that no anarchist or communist centers had been opened there. I searched in detail to see if some of the apostles of libertarian violence – as Osvaldo Bayer called them – had found refuge in the labyrinth before being taken to the prison in Ushuaia or before a firing squad, but their lives had been spent in more central parts of Buenos Aires.

Since the neighborhood seemed so elusive, I went to get to know it. Early one morning I boarded a bus that went from Constitución to Triunvirato Avenue. I headed west and penetrated into terra incognita. When I got to Cádiz Street, the landscape changed into a succession of circles – if circles can be successive – and suddenly I didn't know where I was. I walked for two hours without getting anywhere. At every bend I saw the name of a city: Geneva, The Hague, Dublin, London, Marseilles, Constantinople, Copenhagen. The houses were side by side, with no spaces in between, but the architects had devised a way to make straight lines look curved, or vice versa. Although some had pink lintels and others blue porches – there were also smooth façades, painted white – it was hard to tell them apart: several houses would have the same number, 184 for example, and I thought I saw the same curtains and the same dog poking his muzzle out the window of more than one of the houses. I walked beneath the pitiless sun without crossing paths with a single soul. I don't know how I came out to a plaza enclosed by a black railing. Until then I'd seen only buildings of one or two stories, but around that square were tall towers, also identical, with soccer flags hanging out the windows. I took a few steps backwards and the towers went out like a match. Again I lost my way in the spirals of low houses. I retraced my route, trying to make every step repeat the ones in the opposite direction, and thus I found the plaza again, although not at the point from which I'd left it, but diagonally across from it. For a moment I thought I was the victim of a hallucination, but the low green awning beneath which I'd stood less than a minute ago shone in the sun three hundred feet away, and in its place a business now appeared that called itself the Sandwich Palace, although in fact it was a kiosk that displayed sweets and soft drinks. It was attended by a teenager in an enormous baseball cap that hid his eyes. I was relieved to finally see a human being who could explain what point of the labyrinth we were in. I decided to ask him for a bottle of mineral water because I was dying of thirst, but before I finished the sentence the kid said 'There isn't any,' and disappeared behind a curtain. For a while I clapped my hands to get his attention until I realized that he wouldn't come back as long as I was there.

Before leaving, I'd photocopied a very detailed map of Parque Chas from the Lumi guide, which showed the ways in and out. On the map there was a grey area that might have been a plaza, but its shape was an irregular rectangle and not a square like the one in front of me. Unlike the narrow streets I'd walked along before, these ones had no plaques with street names or numbers on the houses, so I resolved to advance in a straight line from the kiosk towards the west. I had the sensation that, the more I walked, the more the sidewalk lengthened, as if I were moving on an endless ribbon.

It was noon according to my watch and the houses I passed were shut and, it seemed, empty. I had the impression that time was also shifting in a capricious way, like the streets, but I didn't care anymore whether it was six in the afternoon or ten in the morning. The weight of the sun became unbearable. I was dying of thirst. If I saw signs of life in any house, I'd knock and knock, not stopping until someone appeared with a glass of water.

I began to see shadows moving in one of the side streets, miles away from me, and I felt so weak I feared I might faint right there, with no one to help me. I soon saw the shadows weren't hallucinations but dogs that were, like me, looking for somewhere to get a drink and some shade, along with a woman who, at a quick pace, was trying to get past them. The woman was coming towards me but she didn't seem to have noticed my existence, and I didn't notice anything about her other than the sound of her metal bracelets, which months later would have allowed me to identify her even in the dark, because they always moved at the same rhythm, first a quick jangling of metal and then two slow diapasons. I tried to call her so she could tell me where we were – I deduced that she knew because she was walking decisively – but before I could open my mouth, she vanished through a doorway. That sign of life gave me strength to keep going. I walked past two other houses with no one in them and then a façade of sandblasted bricks, with a window grille in the shape of a clover. Contrary to my expectations, there was also a double door, one side of which was open. I went in. I found myself in a spacious, dark room, with a few sports trophies gleaming on shelves, some plastic chairs and two or three framed moralistic mottoes, with phrases like *Quality comes from doing things well just once* and *Perfection is in the details but perfection is no detail.*

Later I found out that the decoration of the room changed in accordance with the mood of the manager, and that sometimes, instead of chairs, there was a counter, and bottles of gin on the shelves, but it's possible that I'm confusing the place with another I went to later, that same day. The scenery in both changed without warning, like in a play. I don't remember very much of what happened next because reality was getting blurred and everything I experienced seemed like part of a dream. Even now I'd still think Parque Chas was an illusion if it wasn't for the fact that the woman I'd seen an instant earlier was in the room and because I saw her again elsewhere many other times.

You're dizzy, was the first thing the woman said to me. Sit down and don't move till you feel better.

I just want a drink of water, I said. My tongue was completely dry and I couldn't say anything else.

From out of the darkness emerged a tall, pale man, with two or three days' growth of very dark beard. He was wearing a tank top and pajama bottoms, and he fanned himself with a piece of cardboard. He approached me with short little steps, avoiding the blinding light from the street.

I don't have a permit to sell water, he said. Only soft drinks and soda water.

Whatever, the woman said to him.

She spoke with such authority it was impossible not to

obey her. Perhaps confused by the sunstroke, at that moment she seemed a woman of irresistible beauty, but when I knew her better I realized she was merely striking. She had something in common with those film actresses one falls in love with for unfathomable reasons, women like Kathy Bates or Carmen Maura or Anouk Aimée or Helena Bonham Carter, who aren't anything out of this world but who make anyone who looks at them feel happy.

She waited while I slowly drank the soda the man in the undershirt offered me, at an exorbitant price, ten pesos, which the woman forced me not to pay – If you give him two pesos, that's already three times as much as it's worth, she said – and then, in an offhand way, asked for a walking stick with a mother-of-pearl handle that must have been left there over a week ago. The man retrieved the object from one of the shelves, where it was hidden behind the trophies. The handle was curved and shiny. Beneath the mother-of-pearl inlays I noticed the traditional image of Carlos Gardel, which adorned the buses in Buenos Aires, wearing a gaucho outfit and white scarf at his throat. It looked like such a unique piece that I asked if I could touch it.

It's not going to wear out, said the woman. The owner almost never uses it anymore.

The walking stick was as light as a feather. The wood was well carved and the image of Gardel could only be the work of a master craftsman. My pondering was interrupted by the man in the undershirt, who wanted to close the club – he said – and go get some sleep. I was feeling better now and asked the woman if she wouldn't mind if we walked out of the labyrinth together as far as a bus stop.

I've got a taxi waiting at the corner of Triunvirato, she said. I can lead you that far.

Although a map with several spots marked on it was sticking out of her handbag, she didn't seem to need it. She didn't make a single wrong turn. As we started walking she asked me my name and what I was doing there.

It's strange to see someone in Parque Chas who's not from the neighborhood, she said. In general, no one ever comes here or leaves.

I repeated what Bonorino had told me about the unexpected Julio Martel recital on one of the corners. I told her how I'd been passionately searching for the singer for months.

It's a shame we didn't meet earlier, she said, as if it were the most natural thing in the world. I live with Martel. I could have introduced you. The cane I came to pick up is his.

I looked at her beneath the scorching light. I realized then that this was the same woman I'd seen on México Street getting into a taxi with the singer. As incredible as it seemed, I had found her in a labyrinth, where everything gets lost. I thought she was tall, but she wasn't. Her stature increased when compared with Martel's negligible size. She had thick, dark hair and the sun didn't affect her: she walked through the elements as if she too were made of light, without getting out of breath.

You could introduce me now, I said hesitantly. I beg you.

No. He's ill now. He came to sing in Parque Chas with an internal hemorrhage and we didn't know it. He sang three tangos, too many. When we left, he fainted in the car. We took him to the hospital and he's had complications. He's in intensive care.

I need to speak with him, I insisted. Whenever he can. I'm going to wait in the hospital until you call me. I'm going to stay right there, if that's all right.

You can do what you like, as far as I'm concerned. It could be weeks, or months, before they let anyone see Martel. It's not the first time it's happened. I've lost count of the number of days I've spent without sleeping.

The curved streets went on monotonously. If someone had asked me where we were, I would have said we were in the same place. I saw the identical curtains in the windows and the same dogs poking out their muzzles. When we turned a corner, however, the landscape changed and straightened out again. During that short walk, I told her what I could about myself, trying to interest the woman in Borges' reflections on the origins of the tango. I told her I'd come to Buenos Aires to work on my dissertation and that, when my money ran out, I'd have no choice but to return to New York. I tried to worm out of her – in vain – how much Martel knew about the original tangos, from singing them and, in his way, composing them all over again. I told her that I couldn't resign myself to all that knowledge dying with him. By then we'd come to Triunvirato Avenue. The taxi was waiting in front of a pizzeria.

Martel is in the Fernández Hospital on Bulnes Street, she

said, in a motherly voice. Visiting hours for intensive care are in the evening, from six-thirty to seven-thirty. I don't think you'll be able to talk to him, but I'll be there all the time.

She closed the door of the taxi and the vehicle moved off. I saw her vague profile through the glass, a hand waving goodbye indifferently, and a smile extinguished by the midday sun, or the sun of whatever time of day it was. I smiled back and at that moment realized I didn't even know her name. I ran down the middle of the avenue, avoiding vehicles moving at full speed, and barely managed to catch up with her at a set of traffic lights. Almost out of breath, I told her what I'd forgotten.

Oh, I'm so distracted, she answered. My name is Alcira Villar.

Now that fate was on my side, I couldn't let her slip through my fingers. I was raised by a Presbyterian family whose first commandment was to work. My father believed that good luck was a sin, because it discouraged effort. I never met anyone who'd won the lottery or who felt happiness was a gift rather than an injustice. Nevertheless, good luck arrived in my life one random morning, at the beginning of summer, six thousand miles south of my birthplace. My father would have ordered me to close my eyes and flee from that temptation. Alcira, I said, Alcira Villar. I couldn't think of anything else or pronounce any other name.

Starting on the following afternoon I stationed myself daily, from six o'clock, in a room adjacent to the intensive care unit. Sometimes I peered out into the corridor and watched the swinging door that opened onto a long hallway, beyond which were the patients, on the second floor of the hospital. The place was clean and bright and nothing interrupted the dense silence of those of us who were waiting. Through the windows we could see a patio with flowerbeds. Sometimes the doctors came in, called some relatives and stood apart speaking to them quietly. I'd follow them when they left to ask how Julio Martel was doing. 'Coming along, coming along,' was all I could get out of them. The nurses took pity on my worry and tried to console me. 'Don't worry, Cogan,' they said, mistreating my name. 'People in intensive care have no reason to die. The majority move into the common wards and then end up going home.' I pointed out that Martel was not there for the first time and that wasn't a good sign. Then they shook their head and admitted: 'True. It's not the first time.'

Frequently, Alcira came to sit with me or asked me to come with her to one of the cafés on Las Heras Avenue. We could never talk in peace, whether it was her mobile phone ringing with offers of research projects, which she invariably turned down, or because handfuls of demonstrators were constantly filing by asking for food. When we found an out of the way table, we were always interrupted by beggars with babies in their arms, or droves of little kids tugging at my pant leg and the sleeves of my shirt so I'd give them a sugar cube, the rancid cookie that came with the coffee or a coin. I eventually became indifferent to the poverty because, almost without noticing, I was turning poor as well.

Alcira, on the other hand, treated them gently, as if they were her brothers lost in some storm and, if a waiter threw them out of the café rudely – which almost always happened – she protested angrily and wouldn't want to stay there another minute.

Although I had about seven thousand dollars accumulated in the bank, I could only withdraw two hundred and fifty per week, after trying my luck at automatic teller machines that were very far apart, more than an hour's bus journey between them. I gradually learned that some banks replenished the funds in their machines at five in the morning and ran out two hours later, and others began the cycle at midday, but thousands of people learned this at the same time as I did and, more than once, after leaving Chiclana Avenue in Boedo, by the time I got to Balbín Avenue, on the other side of the city, the line would already be dispersing because the money had run out. It never took me less than seven hours to get the two hundred and fifty pesos the government allowed, and I couldn't imagine how people who worked regular hours managed.

When my diligence with the banks was successful, I'd pay off my hotel bill and buy a bouquet of flowers for Alcira. She rarely slept and her wakefulness had dulled her gaze, but she concealed her tiredness and looked alert and energetic. Strange as it may seem, no one visited her in the hospital on Bulnes Street. Alcira's parents were very old and lived in some tiny village in Patagonia. Martel was alone in the world. He was a legendary womanizer but had never married, just like Carlos Gardel.

In the room next to the intensive care unit, Alcira told me fragments of the story the singer had gone to Parque Chas to recover, where he'd arrived already hemorrhaging internally. Although I noticed he was weak – she said – he was very animated as he discussed that afternoon's repertoire with Sabadell. I asked him just to sing two tangos but he insisted it had to be three. The previous night he'd explained to me in great detail just what that neighborhood meant to him, he played around with the word neighborhood, 'hood, hard, hoodoo, blood, flood, pub, hero, and I guessed these games hid some tragedy and that nothing in the world was going to keep him from the rendezvous with himself in Parque Chas. However, I didn't realize how bad he was until he fainted, after the last tango. His voice had flowed energetically though somehow sounding both offhand and melancholy, I don't know how to describe it, perhaps because the voice carried with it all his deceptions, happiness, complaints against God and bad luck for his illnesses, everything he had never dared to say in front of people. In the tango, the beauty of the voice is just as important as the way it's sung, the space between the syllables, the intention contained in each phrase. You'll have noticed by now that a tango singer is, first and foremost, an actor. Not just any actor, but someone in whom the listener recognizes his own feelings. The grass that grows over this field of music and lyrics is the wild, rugged, invincible grass of Buenos Aires, the scent of weeds and alfalfa. If the singer were Javier Bardem or Al Pacino with the voice of Pavarotti, you wouldn't be able to endure a single verse. You know how Gardel triumphed with his courteous but common voice where Plácido Domingo failed. The Italian could have been his teacher but when singing *Rechiflao en mi tristeza* he's still Alfredo from *La Traviata*. Unlike those two, Martel doesn't concede the slightest simplicity. He doesn't soften the syllables the melody slides over. You join the drama of what he's singing, as if he were the actors, the scenery, the director and the music of a tear-jerker.

It was, is, summertime, as you know, Alcira said. You could hear the heat crackling. Martel was dressed in his formal clothes for performing in clubs that afternoon. He wore a pair of pinstripe pants, a black double-breasted jacket, a white shirt buttoned up to the collar and one of his mother's scarves, which resembled Gardel's. He'd put on shoes with heels that made walking even more difficult than usual, and makeup on his cheeks and over the bags under his eyes. That morning he asked me to dye his hair black and press his shorts. I used a colorfast dye and brilliantine that keeps the hair dry and shiny. He was afraid that when he sweated, trickles of black would drip down his forehead, like Dirk Bogarde in the last scene of *Death in Venice*.

Parque Chas is a peaceful place, said Alcira. Whatever happens in any part of the neighborhood is instantly known in all the other parts. Gossip is the Ariadne's thread that goes through the infinite walls of the labyrinth. The car bringing us stopped at the corner of Bucarelli and Ballivian, beside a three-story house painted a strange, very pale shade of ochre that seemed to burn in the last of the evening light. Like so many other lots around there, the space it occupied was triangular. There were eight windows on the second floor and two at street level, plus three windows on the terrace. The main door was sunk back into the vertex of the beveled front, like the uvula in a deep throat. Opposite was one of those shops that exist only in Buenos Aires, *galletiterias*, or cookie shops. In prosperous times, they displayed cookies of the most unusual varieties, from ginger stars to cubes filled with asphodel honey to jasmine rings, but Argentine decadence had degraded them, turning them into places to buy soda pop, candies and combs. Past Ballivian, Bucarelli Street sloped upwards, one of the few spots that interrupted the flatness of the city. Two recently painted bits of graffiti declared 'MASSACRE IN PALESTINE' and, under a benevolent image of Jesus, 'IT'S SO NICE TO BE WITH YOU.'

As soon as Sabadell took his guitar out of the case, the apparently deserted streets began to fill up with unexpected people, Alcira said: bowls players, lottery ticket sellers, matrons with curlers askew in their hair, cyclists, accounts clerks with shiny sleeves and the young Korean girls from the cookie shop. The ones who brought folding chairs arranged them in a semicircle in front of the ochre house. Few had ever seen Martel and perhaps none of them had heard him. The few known images of the singer that had appeared in the newspaper *Crónica* and the weekly *El Periodista*, bore not the slightest resemblance to the swollen and aged figure who arrived in Parque Chas that evening. Some applause fell from one of the windows and most of the people joined in. A woman asked him to sing

Cambalache (Junk Shop) and another insisted on *Yira, yira,* but Martel raised his arms and said: 'I'm sorry. I don't have any of Discépolo's tangos in my repertoire. I've come to sing other lyrics, to evoke a friend.'

I don't know if you ever read any stories about Aramburu's death, Alcira said. It would be impossible. Pedro Eugenio Aramburu. Why would you know anything about that, Bruno, in your country, where no one knows anything about the outside world? Aramburu was one of the generals who overthrew Perón in 1955. For the next two years he was the de facto president, allowing the execution without trial of twenty-seven people and ordering the corpse of Eva Perón to be buried on the other side of the ocean. In 1970, he was preparing to return to power. A handful of young Catholics, brandishing the cross of Jesus Christ and the flag of Perón, kidnapped him and condemned him to death at a country estate in Timote. The ochre house was one of the safe houses where the plot was hatched. Mocho Andrade, who had been Martel's playmate, was one of the conspirators, but no one knew that. He fled leaving no trace, no memories, as if he'd never existed. Four years later he showed up at Martel's house, told his version of events, and the next time he disappeared, it was forever.

It was hard to follow Alcira's tale, interrupted by the singer's sudden relapses in the intensive care unit. They kept him going with a respirator and continuous blood transfusions. What I've written down in my notes is a puzzle, the clarity of which I'm not sure.

Andrade, el Mocho, was sturdy, enormous, dark like the

singer, but with unmanageable hair and the high-pitched voice of a hyena. His mother helped Señora Olivia with her sewing work and, when the women got together in the afternoons, Mocho had no choice but to play with the invalid Estéfano. They usually played cards or shared the novels they borrowed from the Villa Urquiza municipal library. Estéfano was a voracious reader. While Mocho spent two weeks reading *In Search of the Castaways*, Estéfano would take one to read *The Mysterious Island* and *Twenty Thousand Leagues Under the Sea*, which were double the number of pages. It was Mocho who investigated the kiosks in Parque Rivadavia and on Corrientes Street where back issues of *20th-Century Songbirds* were going moldy and it was also he who convinced his mother, Señora Olivia and a neighbour to take another ride on the ghost train while Estéfano was recording *El bulín de la calle Ayacucho* in the electroacoustic cabin at a funfair.

Just as one of them dreamed of being an elegant, seductive singer, the other wanted to be a heroic photographer. The invalid was discouraged by his stunted legs, his lack of a neck, his embarrassing hump. Mocho's voice was his ruin, still leaping about crowing and cawing at the age of twenty. In November of 1963, along with two other conspirators, he dragged a bust of Domingo Faustino Sarmiento down Libertad Street in the very center of Buenos Aires, shouting through a megaphone: 'Here goes the barbarous murderer of Chacho Peñaloza!' The scene was meant to be insulting: Mocho's voice made it ridiculous. Although he had his camera on a cord around his neck to capture the indignation of the passersby, he was the one whose picture got taken, and printed on the front page of the evening paper *Noticias Gráficas*. By that time, Estéfano was starting to sing in clubs. His friend showed up in the middle of a performance, walked toward the stage and took a couple of flash photos. Then he disappeared. In early autumn 1970, they crossed paths in the Sunderland and sat at a table in the back drinking to old times. Martel was Martel by then and everyone called him that but to Mocho he was still Téfano.

One of these days, he said, I'm going to Madrid and I'll come back in the black airplane with Perón and Evita.

The Generals won't let Perón in, Martel corrected him. And no one knows where Evita's body is, if they didn't just throw it in the sea.

You'll see, insisted Mocho.

Months later, Aramburu was kidnapped by some young men who went to find him at his house. They put him on trial for two days and at dawn on the third day they executed him with a bullet to the heart. For weeks, a vain search for the conspirators went on, until one morning in July the Córdoba branch of this little army, which called itself the Montoneros, decided to take a mountain village called La Calera. The Aramburu kidnapping had been a masterpiece of military strategy; the attack on La Calera, on the other hand, revealed an insurmountable clumsiness. Two of the guerrillas died, others were wounded, and among the documents the police discovered that afternoon were the keys to the Aramburu kidnapping. All the names of the conspirators were deciphered except for one, FAP. The army's investigators assumed these letters to be the acronym of another organization, the Fuerzas Armadas Peronistas, or Peronist Armed Forces, which had invaded the mountains of Taco Ralo, south of Tucumán, two years before. They were, however, the initials of Felipe Andrade Pérez, alias Magic Eye, alias Mocho.

For six months, Andrade had stayed in a room in the ochre house on Bucarelli Street. In meetings that lasted till dawn, he discussed the details of the kidnapping of Aramburu there with the other conspirators. His mission consisted in helping the owner of the house, blind in one eye and partially sighted in the other, to draw the plans of the apartment where the ex-president lived and to photograph the adjacent garage on Montevideo Street, El Cisne bar – that was on the square – and the magazine stand on Santa Fe Avenue, where there were always people. They memorized the photos, took notes and then burned the negatives. Two weeks before the date chosen for the kidnapping, Mocho designed the escape route. It was he who found the clearings where the prisoner should be transferred from one vehicle to another; he was also the one who decided that the second vehicle, a Gladiator truck, would carry a hollow load of alfalfa bales, inside which the captive and his guards would travel. The most important part of that adventure for him was to register with his camera each and every step: Aramburu leaving the building on Montevideo Street guarded by two fake army officers; the terror on his face in the Gladiator; the interrogations at the farm in Timote, where they took him for trial; the pronouncement of the death sentence, the moment of the execution. At the last minute, however, he was ordered to stay in the house on Bucarelli Street, to command the eventual withdrawal. The conspirators recorded every word Aramburu stammered or spoke during those days, but they didn't take photographs. The head of the operation, who was an amateur, tried to get an image of him silhouetted against a white wall, but the film broke as he pressed the shutter for the fifth time and the shots were lost.

Being left at the margin of the operation so disappointed Mocho that he disappeared from Parque Chas without telling anyone, like so many other times. The conspirators feared he might denounce them but he was not by nature a traitor. He stayed in a grotty boarding house, and a week later went back to Bucarelli Street to pick up his clothes. The house was empty. In the photography lab, above the developing tray, he found three photos taken, undoubtedly, by the clumsy and blind owner of the place. He recognized the images instantly, because his comrades had sent them to all the daily newspapers, and some of them were printed on the front page. One showed the two Parker pens, small calendar and tie pin Aramburu had with him when he was captured; another showed his wristwatch; the third, a medal he'd been given by the 5th Infantry Regiment in May of 1955. He thought it was a grave error not to have destroyed the negatives, and burned them on the spot, with his lighter. He didn't notice the small rectangle with the image of the medal that dropped between the almost invisible crack between the developing tray and a rough stone wall. The army's investigators found it there forty days later, when the disaster of La Calera had already given away the keys of the kidnapping.

The story I've told you should have ended at this point, Alcira said, but that's where it actually begins. The day after the episode in Córdoba, when all the newspapers published the names and photos of Aramburu's kidnappers, Mocho showed up at Martel's house and asked for shelter. He didn't say what he was fleeing from or who was after him. He just said: – 'Téfano, if you don't take me in, I'll kill myself.' He was completely changed. He'd dyed his hair blond, but since it was like steel wool, towering over his head, instead of passing unnoticed, he startled people. His fingernails were a suspicious rusty colour from the acid in the developing fluids, and above his lip he had a thick mustache, which resisted the dye. His voice was still unmistakable, but he barely spoke. When he did, it was in a whisper: still high-pitched, piercing like a dying dog.

At that time, Martel was running the pools at the funeral parlor, and living at the edge of the law, worrying that some slighted gambler might turn him in to the police. So he didn't want to know anything either. Señora Olivia hid Mocho in the sewing room, isolated him from the world by keeping the radio on all the time, and waited, calmly, for the arrival of some tragedy, though she didn't know why. Nothing happened. During the following days, Mocho woke up punctually at seven, did some exercises in the patio and shut himself up in the sewing room to read *The*

Brothers Karamazov. He must have read it at least twice, because nothing else distracted him, aside from the news on the radio. When Estéfano came back from the funeral parlor, they played cards, like when they were teenagers, and the singer let him read the lyrics of the prehistoric tangos he'd restored. One night, at the beginning of August, Mocho disappeared without any explanation, as he always did. Estéfano expected him to reappear that Christmas Eve, when Señora Andrade had a massive heart attack and was admitted to the intensive care unit in the Tornú hospital, but even though the television station's solidarity service spread the word, he didn't come to see her or show up for the funeral, two days later. It seemed like the earth had swallowed him up.

In the next few years everything happened. The military government returned Evita's mummy – which was intact in a tomb no one had known about in Milan – to Perón. For a while, the general didn't know what to do with her: finally, he chose to store her in the attic of his house in Madrid. Later he returned to Buenos Aires. While a million people waited for him near Ezeiza airport, rival Peronist factions attacked each other with rifles, pitchforks and knuckle-dusters. A hundred fighters died and the general's plane landed far away from the bonfires. Perón was elected president of the republic for the third time, but he was broken and ill by then, subject to the will of his secretary and astrologer. He governed for nine months, until he collapsed from fatigue. The astrologer and the widow, a dim-witted woman, took the reins of power. In the middle of October in 1974, the Montoneros kidnapped ex-president Aramburu for the second time. They took the coffin out of its majestic mausoleum in the Recoleta Cemetery and demanded, in exchange for its return, that Evita's remains be repatriated. In November, the astrologer traveled secretly to Puerta de Hierro in a special Aerolíneas Argentinas flight and returned with the illustrious mummy. Aramburu's coffin appeared that same morning in a white truck abandoned on Salguero Street.

Alcira told me that the night before the swap, Mocho Andrade showed up at Martel's house just as if he'd never left. He didn't have his hair dyed anymore and he'd shaved off the mustache. Just long sideburns, in the latest style, and very wide bellbottoms. He asked Señora Olivia if she would cook noodles in meat sauce, drank two bottles of wine and whenever they asked him anything he'd break into his midnight rooster voice and sing a few lines of *Caminito: I've come here for the last time, I've come to tell you of my troubles*. He took a shower and asked if they still had lively milongas in the Sunderland on the weekends. That night Martel should have worked a double shift at the funeral parlor but Mocho wouldn't let him go. He ironed his black evening suit and picked out a white shirt while singing out of tune: *Now, on my downhill slide / all hopes gone / I can no longer root them out.*

He wanted to get the story off his chest, Alcira said. The more cheerful he seemed, the more torn up inside he felt at what he'd experienced. Martel got a table in an isolated corner of the Sunderland, away from the crowds, and ordered a bottle of gin.

175

I kidnapped Aramburu, said Mocho after the first drink, in a fresh, smooth voice, as if he'd just put it on. I was involved in the first kidnapping and in the second, of the corpse. But it's all over now. They're going to find the coffin tomorrow morning.

It seemed to Martel that the couples stopped in the middle of the dance floor, that the music dimmed and time froze. He was afraid the people at the neighboring tables would hear, but the tango from the loudspeakers routed all other sounds and, each time the orchestra reached a final chord, Mocho was lighting a cigarette in silence.

They were there until five in the morning, smoking and drinking. At first, the story he told made no sense, but it gradually began to piece together, although Mocho never revealed where he'd been for the last three years nor why, after he'd left the house on Bucarelli Street, the Montoneros allowed him to take part in the second kidnapping, which was even riskier. Part of what Andrade said that night had been published by the perpetrators of the first kidnapping in a Montonero magazine, but the finale of the plot was then unknown and still seems unbelievable.

I'm an adventurer, as you know, military discipline offends me, Mocho said to Martel, and Alcira told me. I've had few friends, and I've gradually lost them all. One of them died at La Calera; two more were lost due to a mistake in a William Morris pizzeria. The women I fell in love with left me, one after the other. Perón abandoned me too, and he left the country to unravel in the hands of a hysterical widow and a murderous wizard. All I have left is you and someone whose name I cannot repeat.

Three months ago I met a poet. Not just any poet. One of the greats. *They say I'm the best poet in the country*, he's written. *They say, and it may well be true.* We got together almost every night in his house in Belgrano, beside the bridge where the train tracks cross Ciudad de la Paz Street. We talked about Baudelaire, René Char and Boris Vian. Sometimes, we played cards, just like you and I used to do in the old days. I knew that, just before Perón's return, the poet had been in Villa Devoto prison, and that he was a legendary militant, mythic: the opposite of mystic, Téfano, a devotee of food, women and gin. Petit bourgeois, I called him. Petit nothing, he'd answer. I am a grand bourgeois.

One night, in his house, after a few drinks, he asked me if I was scared of the dark. I live in the dark, I said. I'm a photographer. The half-light is my element. Not afraid of darkness or death or enclosed spaces. Then you – he said – are one of my men. He'd prepared a perfect plan to steal Aramburu's corpse.

We started at six in the evening, two days later. There were four of us. I never knew, nor will I ever know who the other audacious ones were. We walked into Recoleta Cemetery through the main entrance and hid inside one of the mausoleums. Until one in the morning we didn't move. No one spoke, no one dared to cough. I kept myself occupied by braiding the threads of some cloths I found on the floor. The place was clean. It smelled of flowers. It was the middle of October, a warm night. When we came out of our hiding place, our legs were numb. The silence burned our throats. Twenty steps away, in one of the central avenues, was the Aramburu tomb. Forcing it open and removing the coffin was simple. We had more trouble with the cemetery locks, which made a dreadful noise when we broke them. An owl hooted and flew between the poplars; it seemed like a bad omen. Outside, on Vicente López, a stolen hearse was waiting for us. The street was deserted. The only people to see us were a couple coming out of one of the hourly hotels on Azcuénaga Street. They crossed themselves when they saw the coffin and quickened their pace.

Remember, Alcira said, during those months Isabel and the astrologer López Rega had ordered the construction of an altar for the nation, where they planned to reunite the bodies of the adversarial national leaders. Figueroa Alcorta Avenue was cut off at Tagle, and the cars got tangled up in a detour designed by a cubist city planner. The projected building was a Pharaonic Pyramid: San Martín's mausoleum was going to be at the entrance. Behind it, those of Rosas and Aramburu. On the top of the pyramid, Perón and Evita. Without Aramburu, the project would be incomplete. When the wizard found out one of his corpses had been stolen, he flew into a rage. He sent a mob of policemen out to comb the streets of Buenos Aires in search of the lost body. Who knows how many innocent people were murdered in those days. Aramburu, however, was right there in everyone's sight.

Shortly before the Recoleta operation – Mocho told

Martel, and Alcira repeated to me much later – the poet had seized one of those tanker trucks they use to transport gasoline and kerosene. Don't ask me how he did it, because he didn't tell us. All I know is that for at least a month no one was going to notice it was missing. The truck was new, and the Montoneros' mechanics had cut a door through which you could access the tank from below. At the top, they'd cut three invisible holes that let in air and, sometimes a bit of light. The poet had decided to hide the body there and drive it around the city, in full view of the henchmen. In case of any accidents, we were supposed to protect the trophy with our own lives. One of us would stand guard inside the tank, with an arsenal for emergencies. We planned to each take turns of eight days in the darkness, and forty-eight hours at the wheel of the truck. Sometimes we parked in secure places, other times we drifted around Buenos Aires. The one in the cab had to stay alert. The one who was in the tank had a mattress and a latrine. There were four of us, like I said. We tossed a coin to see when we took our turn in the tank. The poet got the first one. I got the last. By chance, I was to drive for the first forty-eight hours.

The plan went along without the slightest hitch. We took the coffin to the no man's land in between the River Plate stadium and the targets of the Federal rifle club, and there we moved it from the hearse to the tank. The poet allowed me to take photos for five minutes but, before we dispersed, he handed the camera to one of the other comrades.

You'll be able to take all the photos you want when it's your turn to ride inside, he said.

I got up behind the wheel. No one else was in the cab. In the glove compartment I had a nine-millimeter Walther and, within reach of my hand, a walkie-talkie to inform the others, at regular intervals, as to how everything was going. I crossed the city from one extreme to the other, until the early hours. The truck drove well and turned easily. I went down Callao Avenue first, then I took Rodríguez Peña again and headed for Combate de los Pozos, Entre Ríos and Sársfield. It was the first time I'd wandered around with no destination in mind, without deadlines, and I felt that life was only worthwhile like this. When I got as far as Malbrán Institute I turned onto Amancio Alcorta and then headed up north, towards Boedo and Caballito. I drove slowly, to save gas. The streets were full of potholes and it was difficult to avoid jolts. The poet's voice startled me.

There's no better place to write than in the darkness, he said.

I didn't know the tank could communicate with the cab of the truck by way of an almost imperceptible sliver of air that slipped out through an opening behind the latrine.

I'm going to take you to Parque Chas, I said.

May the arrival point be the departure point, he answered. We're always going to be to blame for everything that happens in this world. As the sky began to get light I parked at the corner of Pampa and Bucarelli and got out to buy coffee and some cookies. Then I crossed the railway lines and stopped beside the Communications Club. No one could see us. I opened the entrance to the tank and told the poet to get out and stretch his legs.

You woke me up, he complained.

We're not stopping often, I said. You better get out now instead of when you're going crazy with claustrophobia.

As soon as I saw him walk a few steps away, I took a look around the inside of the tank. In spite of the breathing holes, the air was thick and an acrid, dry odor that resembled no other floated at head height. Rancid remains, I said to myself, although all remains are. Limestone and flowers. I opened the coffin. I was surprised that the protective panel was detached, because when we took him out of the cemetery I hadn't heard the sound of anything loose. The shadow lying there must have been no other than Aramburu: he had a rosary wound round what were once his fingers and, on his chest, he wore the medal of the 5th Infantry Regiment that they'd found in Bucarelli Street. The shroud was frayed and what was left of the body was very little indeed, almost the scraps of a child.

Leaning against one of the mudguards of the truck, the poet was chewing on a cookie.

It makes no sense to go from place to place, he said. I feel like Madame Bovary traveling all night with her lover through the suburbs of Rouen.

I was the driver, I said, but I wasn't as desperate as the one in the novel to stop at an inn.

It would have been better if you'd got out and stayed quiet. I spent the time writing a poem by flashlight. If we take a monotonous route, I'll read it to you.

When we got back on the road, I chose the most

monotonous route I know: General Paz Avenue, the northern and western border of Buenos Aires.

Barely enough light to see, said the poet, from the tank. The batteries are going. Any moment now I'm going to go blind. *I spy / boasting and apocryphal / humility and much / hidden suffering. I spy the shared / light of unknowing, I spy, / with my little eye, a branch, what color: I couldn't say.*

It went on like that. He read the whole poem and then read some others until the flashlight was dim and dying. *I spy and I want to rest / a little, it's understandable.* I can't see very well, he said. About six in the evening we went to fill up with gas at the operations house, we got out for a moment to have a coffee and I felt the weight of the day on my body. I wasn't tired or feeling or wanting anything and I could even have said I was no longer thinking. Only time moved within me in some direction I don't know how to express, time backed away from the childhood without childhood we shared − Mocho Andrade said to Martel, and Alcira repeated to me later, in the first person as it had been passed from one person to the next − and somehow went missing in what was perhaps my old age; we were all so very old in one of time's lost gusts that day.

I watched the poet climb out of the tank looking as old as his father. The proximity of death had unhinged him: a lock of hair fell, as usual, across his forehead, but it was faded and dull, and his wide, ox-like jaw was collapsing. That night we camped in Centenary Park and at dawn the next day I started to drive around Parque Chas where the residents weren't surprised when the truck passed over and over again down the same streets with their names of European cities: Berlin, Copenhagen, Dublin, London, Cádiz, where the landscape, though always the same, had seams of mist or port smells, as if we really were crossing those remote places. Once I got lost in the tangle of streets but this time I did it on purpose, to use up time as I searched for a way out. I followed the curve of Londres Street and without knowing how I was suddenly in Jimmy Joy's dear dirty Dublin, or the truck frolicked in the Tiergarten on its way to the Berlin Wall, waving to the neighbors who remained indifferent, because they were well used to the vehicles becoming disconcerted in Parque Chas and being abandoned by their drivers.

After I left the truck I slept for two days solid, and when I took the wheel again, a week later, the poet had vanished from the tank. I realized that the rounds of the dance meant we wouldn't coincide again until the end, when it was my turn to look after the corpse. At the beginning of November an incandescent sun shone over Buenos Aires. I was waiting to be called in as relief, sleeping in ruined hotels in the Bajo under a false name. Every five hours I phoned the operations house, to let them know I was still alive. I would have liked to see the poet, but I knew it wasn't prudent. I heard that the truck was in motion almost always around the port, blending in with the hundreds of other trucks that came and went from the docks, and that life inside the tank was getting intolerable. Perhaps Aramburu had also found another hell in that perpetual voyage.

Early one morning, around three, they came to get me so

I could serve my sentence of eight days inside the tank. I had already packed my backpack with two cameras, twelve rolls of film, two strong lamps with replacement batteries and a thermos of coffee. They had warned me not to take photos at night, and if the sun stopped shining through the breathing holes at any point during the day I was to interrupt any work immediately. I tried not to retch as I entered the tank. Even though they'd just cleaned and disinfected it, the smell was venomous. I felt like I was in one of those caves where moles collect insects and worms. As well as the gravitational force that death imposed on the air, there was the organic smell of the bodies that had preceded me and the memory of the excrement they'd expelled. The ghosts did not want to withdraw. How had the poet been able to find his voice in that darkness? *I am about to open the doors*, he'd written, *to close / my eyes and not look / further than my nose, not smell, not take the name of God in vain*.

I lay down, prepared to sleep until daybreak. The mattress had formed humps and ravines, the surface was slightly sticky, I didn't want to complain, I didn't feel that it was the end of youth. I woke up a short while later because the truck was bumping around, as if the comrade at the wheel was driving carelessly over a muddy road. I approached the ventilation slit and said:

Do you want me to sing to amuse you? I have a unique voice. I was a soloist in choir at school.

If you want to help me, don't talk and don't sing, came the answer. It was a girl. You don't have the voice of a person, you screech like a bug.

One of the other two from the cemetery had begun the journey with me. I didn't know when the girl had replaced him. Or maybe there were two people in the cab.

Are there two of you? I wanted to know. And the poet? Does he have a turn to drive on this leg of the journey?

No one said anything. I felt like the last survivor on earth.

We kept going around, without ever stopping. Every once in a while I heard airplane engines, the quick rattling of trains and dogs barking. I didn't even know where I was when the sun came out and I fixed the two lamps on projections on opposite sides of the truck so that, when lit, the light would shine directly onto the corpse. The person who was at the wheel of the truck, whoever it might be, was not a great driver. We hit every pothole and all the uneven bits in the road. I was afraid that with so many jolts I wouldn't be able to turn off the lamps in time if we went through any darkened areas.

I'm going to turn on some lights back here, I warned, through the ventilation crack. Knock twice when we're approaching a tunnel.

There were two knocks, but sunlight kept pouring through the holes for ten, fifteen minutes. I drank some hot coffee and ate two buns. Then, I checked my pulse. I needed to keep the aperture open, without trembling, for at least five seconds. I illuminated the dingy space. Only then did I notice that beneath Aramburu's body was another, in a wooden packing crate. It was slightly bigger and wasn't wearing any medals or rosaries, but the shroud that covered it was almost identical. If I hadn't seen the real remains a few weeks earlier I wouldn't have been able to tell who was who, and even now I had my doubts. I took at least three full rolls of photos of both corpses, close-ups and long shots. When I developed them I'd be sure. After an hour and a half I went back to the mattress. Who knows how long we'd been driving without a break. It couldn't be much longer before we'd go back to the operations house. Suddenly, we glided down a slope and I realized we were in Parque Chas. After a few circuitous laps, the truck eased into a straight line and left the labyrinth. We went on like that until night fell. I had run out of coffee and food, my legs hurt and my senses were dulled by a dense cloud inside my head. I didn't even notice when we stopped. Since they took their time opening the door of the tank, I shouted and shouted, but no one answered. I was there for a long time, resigned to succumbing in the company of those two dead men. But before dawn they freed me. I could barely stand up in the patio of the operations house, beside the running board of the empty cab. Someone who seemed to be in charge, a short guy with a red beard I'd never seen before, pointed me towards a straw mattress in the attic and ordered me not to come down from that floor until they called me. I thought I'd fall asleep on the spot, but the fresh air woke me up and, leaning out the window, I contemplated the patio with an empty mind, as the light turned from grey to pink, and then to yellow and the glories of the morning. A girl with a thicket of dark curls approached the truck, shaking off the water from the shower like a puppy, and examined the contents of the tank. I guessed she was the one who had been traveling in the cab, and felt a flash of embarrassment because, suffocated into stupidity, I'd forgotten to remove my excrement. It was mid-morning by the time a white van parked beside the tank. My exhaustion was getting the better of me but I was there, awake, unable to tear my eyes away from the patio, where the tiles looked scorching. I suppose there must have been a street or a field beyond, I don't know. Now I'll never know. Three men I didn't know took Aramburu's coffin out of the tank: I recognized it, because I'd taken a sickening number of photographs of the crucifix on the lid, with its golden halo above Christ's open arms and, underneath, the succinct plaque with the general's name and years of birth and death. The girl with the ringlets ordered each of the corpse's movements: Put it on one side, on the platform, slowly, don't scratch the wood. Uncover it. Leave what's inside on top of the bed. Slowly, slowly. Nothing should be out of place.

My torpor lifted as soon as I discovered what was happening. You'd have to have an iron stomach not to be horrified by those two open coffins – one luxurious, imperial; the other miserable, badly made, like the ones hurriedly assembled in cities with the plague – and by the ruins of the two dead bodies lying in the open air. The girl with the ringlets arranged something that, from my vantage point in the attic, looked like a swap, although I don't know now if what I saw was what I think I saw or if it was just a trick of my senses, the embers of the days I spent shut up in the tank. With the fastidiousness of cabinetmakers they took the rosary and one of the military medals from one of the bodies, and put them on the chest and between the fingers of the other corpse. What had been in one of the coffins was taken to the other and vice versa, I'm not sure about what I'm saying – Mocho told him, and Alcira repeated it to me, and I am telling it in turn in a language that undoubtedly has very little in common with the original tale, none of the tremulous syntax or the unwrinkled voice that lasted a few hours in Mocho's throat, that distant night in the Sunderland – I'm only sure that the luxurious coffin went into the white van and the miserable one went back into the tanker, perhaps with a different body inside.

I slept the whole morning and woke up around one o'clock. There was an enormous silence in the house and, call as I might, I didn't see anyone. At about two, the poet appeared at the door where they'd confined me. I embraced him. He was thin, shaken, as if surfacing from a grave illness. I began to tell him what I'd seen and he told me to be quiet, to forget it, that things are never what they appear to be. *I'm not from here anymore*, he recited: *I barely feel like a passing memory. Neither you nor I are of this unhappy world, to which we give our lives so that nothing remains as it is.* It's time to go, he said.

He covered my eyes with a black cloth and dark glasses. That's how I left the operations house, blindfolded, leaning on his shoulder. For more than an hour I was led along paths that smelled of cows and wet grass. After that, I was surrounded by a persistent stink of gas. We stopped. The poet's hand removed the sunglasses and black blindfold. The sun was shining straight down on us and my eyes took a long time to adjust. I made out, a hundred meters away, the tanks and towers of an oil refinery. There was a long line of tanker trucks identical to the one I knew at the entrance, while other also identical ones drove out every five minutes or so. We stood in silence for I don't know how long, contemplating that rhythmic and tedious coming and going.

Are we going to stay here all day? I said. I thought the work was finished.

One never knows when something finishes.

At that very instant our truck drove out of the refinery. It was too familiar an image not to recognize. They'd also painted an imperceptible yellow line over the door of the tank and, from where we stood, we saw the line gleaming as a ray of sun struck it.

Should we follow it? I asked.

We'll just let it disappear into the distance, the poet said. *Until the ashes are blown away on the wind.*

We lost sight of the imposing cylinder on the highway, laden with its small lake of gasoline. It carried a body that would disintegrate as the years went by and leave strands of itself in the subterranean tanks of the service stations and, through the tailpipes of cars, in the air without flair of Buenos Aires.

I'll give you a lift. Where are you going? the poet asked.

Drop me off anywhere near Villa Urquiza. I'm going to walk.

I wanted to think about what I'd done and what it meant, to know whether I was fleeing something or going towards something. *My confidence rests on the profound disdain for this unhappy world*, the poet had said to me. *I'll give my life so that nothing remains as it is*. We spend our lives giving them up for causes we don't entirely understand only so that nothing will remain as it is, Mocho said to Martel that night in the Sunderland.

Couples danced indifferently around them. An entourage of moths fluttered around the spotlights. Some brushed against the burning glass and died. Martel was perturbed for a long time. The wings of history had brushed against Mocho and he too heard the sound of flight. It was more vehement than the music, more dominant and intense than the sound of the city. It had to embrace the whole country and the next day, or the following, it would be on the front page of the papers. He felt like saying, as his mother did when confronted with a death, 'What tiny things we are, nothing at all in eternity,' but he just said: 'That's the only reason I sing as well: so what once was returns and nothing remains as it is.'

The next morning, Alcira told me, Mocho wanted Martel to accompany him to the house on Bucarelli Street, where the labyrinth of his own life had begun. The radios announced the return of Evita's corpse and the discovery of the white van with Aramburu's coffin inside. If what Andrade wanted to do was to finish one story and go back to the past to begin again – as he said to the singer in the Sunderland – he had no choice but to return to Parque Chas and hold a vigil over the ruins of his life.

Their morning was a series of disappointments, one after

the other. The conspirators' house had been cordoned off and a patrol car stood guard by the door. In the distance, the streets opened in circles and on the sidewalks that stopped without warning there was not a soul to be seen and the silence was so oppressive it was hard to breathe. Not even the dogs stuck their noses out between the curtains. They couldn't stop to look up at the windows of the top floor without appearing suspicious to the police in the patrol car, so they turned onto Ballivian in the direction of Bauness and back up the slope that came out on Pampa. Every once in a while, Martel turned to Mocho and detected his growing despair. He would have liked to take his arm, but he feared that any gesture, the lightest touch, and his friend would dissolve into tears.

When they got to the bus stop, Andrade said they had to part company at this point because he was expected somewhere else, but Martel knew that somewhere else was nowhere, perdition, that he had no one left to ask for refuge. He didn't even try to keep him from going. Mocho seemed in too much of a hurry and detached himself from his embrace as if he were detaching from himself.

He had no more news of him until eleven years later, when one of the survivors of the dictatorship mentioned in passing that a big man with the voice of a rooster had been 'transferred' one summer's night from the dungeons of the Athletic Club, that is, taken to his death. The witness didn't even know the real name of the victim, only his *noms de guerre*, Rubén or Magic Eye, but the mention of the voice was enough for Martel. The name Felipe Andrade Pérez does not figure on any of the infinite lists of disappeared persons that have circulated since then, nor is it recorded in the civil actions against the dictatorship's commanders, as if he'd never existed. The story he'd told in the Sunderland was, however, full of meaning for Martel. It represented what he himself would have wanted to experience if he'd been able to, and also – although he was less sure about this – it represented the rebel's death he wished he could have had. That was why, Alcira said, he dyed his hair black, with the illusion of returning to his self of twenty-seven years ago, and put on his striped pants and black double-breasted recital jacket, and went out one evening two weeks ago to evoke his friend on the corner of Bucarelli and Ballivian, in front of the house they hadn't been able to enter the last time they'd seen each other.

Accompanied by Sabadell's guitar, Martel sang *Sentencia*, by Celedonio Flores. In spite of the makeup over the bags under his eyes and on his cheeks, he was pale, full of rage against the body that had abandoned him when he most needed it. I thought he was going to faint, said Alcira. He squeezed his abdomen tightly, as if holding up something that was falling, and went on like that: *I was born, your honor, in the back streets / unhappy back streets of immense sorrow*. The tango is a long one, lasting more than three and a half minutes. I feared he wouldn't be able to finish it. The little Korean girls from the cookie shop applauded him as they would have applauded a sword swallower. Three boys rode by on their bikes, shouted 'Encore!' and went on. Maybe the scene seems pathetic to you, said Alcira, but in reality it was almost tragic: the greatest Argentine singer opening his wings for the last time before people who didn't know what was happening.

Sabadell amused himself for a while on the guitar, jumping from a fragment of *La cumparsita* to others from *Flor de fango (Flower of Mud)* and *La morocha (The Brunette)*, until he got to *La casita de mis viejos (My Folks' Little House)*. More than once Martel was on the verge of collapsing into sobs as he sang that tango. His throat must have hurt, perhaps a memory was hurting him too, the memory of a dead man who didn't want to accept his condition, like all those who have no grave. Why didn't he cry, then? Alcira said to herself and later said to me, in the hospital on Bulnes Street. Why did he hold back the tears that might well have saved him? *Quiet neighborhood of my past / like a melancholy dusk / on your corner I grow old . . .*

He was sweating buckets. I told him we should go – Alcira told me – I stupidly told him that Felipe Andrade would have surely sung along with him by now from his eternity, but he rebuffed me with a firmness or fierceness I'd never seen in him before. He said: 'If there were two tangos for the rest of them, why should there also be only two tangos for my dearest friend.'

He had obviously discussed the subject with Sabadell, because the guitarist interrupted me with the prelude to *Como dos extraños (Like Two Strangers)*. The lyrics of that song conjure up a spell against the pure past that Martel was trying to resuscitate, Alcira told me. That afternoon, however, a past that was not dead flowed through Martel's voice, the way something cannot be dead when it has only disappeared and remains and endures. The past of that afternoon kept tenaciously in the present while he sang: it was the nightingale, the first lark from the world's beginnings, the mother of all songs. I still can't understand how he could have breathed, where he got the strength to keep from fainting. I found myself crying when I heard him sing, for the second time: *And now I stand before you / we seem like two strangers / a lesson I've learned at last. / How the years do change things!* I myself was remembering things I'd never lived.

With the last word of *Como dos extraños* Martel collapsed, while the people of Parque Chas asked for yet another tango. When he fell into my arms I heard him say, with the last of his strength: 'Get me to the hospital, Alcira, I've nothing left. I'm dying.'

I don't remember if Alcira told me that episode the last time I visited her in the Fernández Hospital or weeks later, in the Café La Paz. I only remember that midnight in December with the sky in flames, and Alcira by my side, exhausted, standing before the nurse who was trying to console her and didn't know how, and the silence that passed over the waiting room, and the smell of rotting flowers that took the place of reality.

SIX

December 2001

During those insane days I bought some maps of Buenos Aires and drew colored lines on them joining the places where Martel had sung, in the hope of finding some picture that might decipher his intentions, something like the rhombus with which Borges solves the riddle in 'Death and the Compass.' The imperfect geometric figures varied, as we know, according to the order in which the points connect. Starting from the boarding house where I'd lived, on Garay Street, I could uncover the outline of a mandrake, or a slightly twisted Y that resembled geomancy's *Caput Draconis*, or even a mandala similar to Eliphas Lévi's magic circle. I saw what I wanted to see.

I carried my maps around everywhere and sketched new drawings when I got bored of reading in cafés. I traced lines between the places where, according to Virgili, the bookseller, Martel had sung before I arrived in Buenos Aires: the lovers' hotels on the Azcuénaga Street, next to Recoleta Cemetery, the subterranean tunnel under the obelisk in the Plaza de la República. In the newspaper archive in the National Library – the one where Grete Amundsen had got lost months before – I looked for evidence of why Martel might have chosen those spots. The only stories I found were of a couple murdered in the act in a hotel that rented rooms by the hour, towards the end of the sixties, and that of an execution by firing squad at the obelisk during the first months of the dictatorship. There didn't seem to be any connection between the events. The murderer in the hotel was a jealous husband whom the police had alerted by phone, back when adulterers were denounced. He wasn't even tried: three doctors certified that he'd been temporarily deranged and the judge absolved him a few months later. And the death at the obelisk was one more of so many between 1976 and 1980. Despite being a ferocious exhibition of impunity, not a single Argentine daily paper registered the fact. I found the piece of information by chance in the *Economist*, where the Buenos Aires correspondent wrote that one Sunday in June 1976 – the 18th, I think – a group of men in steel helmets arrived at the Plaza de la República slightly before dawn in an unmarked car. An unidentified young person was dragged across the plaza, leaned up against the white granite of the enormous obelisk and shot with a burst of machine-gun fire. The murderers left in the same car, abandoning the corpse, and nothing more was known.

I gradually began to realize that, as long as I didn't know where else in Buenos Aires Martel had sung, I would never manage to complete the pattern – if there was any pattern – and I didn't dare bother Alcira with something that might only be a crazy idea. When I asked if she knew where else

Martel had performed for himself, apart from the places we already knew, she, upset about what was going on in the intensive care unit, just mumbled a few names: Mataderos, the tunnels, the Waterworks Palace, and left. I'm trying to remember, she answered me once. I'll write down a list of places and give it to you. She didn't do so until much later, when I was about to leave Buenos Aires.

Many of my afternoons were empty, poisoned by in-difference. As Christmas approached I kept telling myself it was time to go home. I'd received a few cards from friends regretting my absence at Thanksgiving, at the end of November. Busy trying to imagine how to get Bonorino out of the cellar of the aleph, the holiday had passed me by unnoticed. My head was all over the place and it was starting to worry me. At this rate, I thought, my grants will run out before I've written even a third of my dissertation.

I read that they were going to show *Tango!*, billed as 'our first talkie', on the smallest screen at the San Martín, where I'd seen some of the masterpieces of Argentine cinema. The work dated from 1933, when six years had already gone by since Al Jolson sang in *The Jazz Singer*. I guessed the information was probably incorrect. And it was. In the two years before a couple of talking melodramas had been filmed, like *Buenos Aires Baby Dolls*, with records that attempted in vain to synchronize the dialogues with the images. What matters, however, is that when I saw *Tango!* I was convinced that it had been Argentina's farewell to the silent era.

The plot was innocuous, and the only interesting thing

was a succession of duos, trios, quintets and orchestras, which stopped playing every once in a while so the actors could recite their lines. *The Jazz Singer* had contributed an immortal phrase to the cinema, *You ain't heard nothing yet.* In the first scene of *Tango!*, a robust female singer, disguised as a bad guy, opened fire with a line that instantly unleashed a storm of meanings: *Buenos Aires, cuando lejos me vi,* when I'm far away. So, the first sound uttered in Argentine cinema had been that pair of words, *Buenos Aires.*

While I distractedly watched the film – the dialogues of which I couldn't follow, I'm not sure whether due to the actors' blurred diction or because the soundtrack must have been very primitive – I was afraid the city would pull away from me one day and nothing would be as it had been anymore. I held my breath, in the hope that the present wouldn't move out of its frame. I ended up feeling nowhere, without a time to cling onto. What I used to be had got lost somewhere and I didn't know how to find it again. The film itself confused me, because it had a circular structure in which everything returned to its starting point, including the fat lady disguised as a bad guy, who reappeared in the final minute, singing a milonga that referred – I think – to Buenos Aires: *I don't know why they mention her to me / when I cannot forget her.*

When I left, as I waited for the 102 bus, which dropped me near the Fernández Hospital, I noticed that something was changing in the city's atmosphere. At first I thought that the afternoon light, always so intense, so yellow, had turned to a pale pink. It seemed like dusk had got ahead of itself. It always got dark at nine in the evening at that time of year. And it was six-thirty. I had the impression that Buenos Aires was changing its mood, and at the same time it seemed absurd to say that about a city. I'd walked through Plaza Vicente López a few days earlier and I didn't recognize it the way I was seeing it at that moment: with some of its trees bare, flat, and others full of flowers that fluttered and fell in slow motion. The municipal gardeners must have sawn off some of their branches from birth, I thought. I didn't understand that cruel and useless custom, which I'd observed in other tree-lined streets and even in the Palermo Forest, where I saw a *palo borracho* murdered by the violence of the pruning.

On one side of Recoleta Cemetery, six living statues were crossing the street with cases in their hands. I thought it strange that they were walking so quickly, unconcerned with the astonishment they were provoking. The illusion of immobility, which was all the grace of their negligible art, vanished with every step. They looked ridiculous in their golden and granite costumes, and with thick layers of paint in their hair and on their faces: an inconceivable carelessness among those who always hid to remove their makeup. Maybe they'd been moved on from the area surrounding the Church of Pilar, where they usually worked, though that had never happened before.

When I got off the bus across from Las Heras park, I saw packs of dogs that had rebelled against the guys who were walking them. In that place atrocious things had gone on, and the hangovers of the horror were still there. To have a break from rushing about with the dogs, their minders would get together to chat in a shady part of the park where in days gone by the courtyard of the National Penitentiary used to be. Each of them held the leads of seven or eight animals, and let one of the dogs loose, the most seasoned, to guide the pack. I don't suppose any of them would have known that the anarchist Severino Di Giovanni was shot by firing squad in that corner in 1931, as well as General Juan José Valle, who, twenty-five years later, had taken up arms to bring Peronism back to power. And if they did know, what would it matter to them? Sometimes the wind blew harder there than in other parts of the park, and the dogs, distressed by a smell they didn't understand – the smell of a human sorrow that came from the past – slipped their leads and ran off. More than once, in my daily trips to the Fernández Hospital, I'd seen the boys chasing them and getting them back together, but that afternoon, instead of running away, the dogs circled around and around their wardens, tangling them up till they fell. The animals who acted as guides rose up on two legs and howled, while the rest of the pack, drooling, stood a few feet off from their fallen walkers and then approached again, as if they wanted to drag them away from that place.

I arrived at the hospital feeling like the city was no longer the same, that I was no longer the same. I feared Martel might have died while I was wasting time at the cinema and I almost ran up the stairs to the waiting room. Alcira was talking calmly to a doctor and, when she saw me, called me over.

He's getting better, Bruno. I went into the room a little while ago and he asked for a hug, and he hugged me with the energy of someone determined to live. He hugged me without worrying about those tubes he's got stuck in his body. Maybe he'll get up, like the times before, and sing again.

The doctor – a short man with a shaved head – patted her on the shoulder.

Let's just wait a few weeks, he said. He still has to detoxify from all the medication we've been pumping into him. His liver isn't helping much.

But this morning he had no strength and look at him now, doctor, Alcira replied. This morning his little arms were limp, he could barely hold up his head, like a new-born. Now he hugged me. Only I know how much life he has to have to hug me like that.

I asked if I could go into Martel's room and sit beside him. I'd been waiting for days for them to let me speak to him.

Not just yet, said the doctor. He's coming around but he's still very weak. Perhaps tomorrow. When you see him, don't ask him questions. Don't say anything that could make him emotional.

Some people were walking through the corridors with headphones on. They must have been listening to the radio because, when they passed each other, they commented excitedly on news that was happening elsewhere: That's three in Rosario now! I heard a woman leaning on a cane in the shape of a tripod say, And what about Cipoletti? See that in Cipoletti? another answered. More dead, my God! a nurse coming down from the third floor commented. I'm going to be stuck in the emergency room all night.

Alcira was afraid there'd be a power cut. At lunchtime, on the television in a bar, she'd seen desperate people ransacking supermarkets and taking food. Thousands of bonfires were lit in Quilmes, in Lanús, in Ciudadela, at the gates of Buenos Aires. No one mentioned disturbances in the city. She asked me if I'd seen any.

Everything seemed calm, I answered. I didn't want to mention the signs of unease that had surprised me: the color of the sky, the living statues.

She was too anxious to carry on a conversation. I found her odd, as if she'd left her body elsewhere. Deep circles under her eyes darkened her face, which expressed nothing, neither thoughts nor emotions. It seemed like everything in her had left with the body that wasn't there.

On my way back to the hotel in the bus, I saw people running through the streets in a state of agitation. Most of them were practically naked. The men had bare chests and wore shorts and flip-flops; the women's blouses were coming undone or their dresses loose and light. At the corner of Callao and Guido an old man, his hair hardened with brilliantine, got on the bus. He would have looked out of place among the other passengers if his suit weren't worn and shiny, the elbows wearing through. When we got to Uruguay Street, a demonstration blocked traffic. The driver tried to force his way through by honking, but the more he called attention to the bus the more the demonstrators pulled together. The old man, who up till that moment had maintained his composure, leaned his head out the window and shouted: Kick those bastards out once and for all! Kick 'em all out! Then he turned to me, on his left, and said excitedly, perhaps proudly: This morning I had the pleasure of stoning the president's automobile. I smashed the windshield. I would have liked to smash his head.

What was happening wasn't just unexpected but incomprehensible to me as well. For weeks people had been complaining about politicians in increasingly violent tones, and some had even been punched, but nothing appeared to change. The attacks on the supermarkets seemed impossible, because the police were patrolling the streets constantly, so I dismissed them as another invention by the television people, who didn't know how to get people's attention anymore. I'd heard only discontented voices since my arrival in Buenos Aires. When it wasn't the weather it was the poverty – which you now saw everywhere, even in streets where you previously saw only prosperity, like Florida and Santa Fe – but it was never more than complaining. Now, the words unleashed into the air had sharp edges and destroyed whoever they named. Kick those bastards out, the people shouted and, although the bastards didn't move, reality was so tense, so ready to crack, that the jolt of the insult pushed the politicians to their downfall. Or at least that's how it seemed to me.

Even the President of the Republic was getting stones thrown at him. Could it be true? Maybe the old man on the bus was boasting, to make himself feel important. If he'd stoned the car and everyone had seen, how could he be sitting there so calmly? Why had nothing happened to him? Sometimes the labyrinth of the city wasn't only in the streets and the temporal confusions for me, but in the unexpected behavior of the people who lived there.

I waited for half an hour and, since the traffic remained at a standstill, I decided to walk. I went up Uruguay as far as Córdoba and then turned down Callao, towards the hotel. I had no desire to return to my suffocating room but I couldn't think where else to go. The shops were closing their shutters, the cafés were deserted, just getting rid of their last clients. Crossing the whole city to take refuge in the Café Británico would be insane. The human tides were unending. Everything was closed but the streets were teeming and I felt as lonely as a dog, if by any chance dogs get lonely. It was late by then, nine or maybe later, and the people going from place to place gave the impression of having just woken up. They were carrying old wooden spoons, pots and pans.

I started to feel hungry and regretted not having bought anything to eat at the hospital. At my hotel they'd closed the blinds and I had to ring the bell over and over again before they'd let me in. The doorman was also wearing nothing but underpants. His enormous torso, with its thickets of hair, gleamed with sweat.

Look at this, Míster Cogan, he said. Look at the disaster that's happened in Constitución.

He had a miniature television on behind the reception desk. They were showing the sacking of a market live.

People were running with bags of rice, cans of oil and strings of sausages, between columns of smoke. An ageless old woman, her face a map of wrinkles, fell with her legs straight out in front of her, by a fan. She began to clean the open wound in her head with one hand as she held her skirt with the other, so the breeze wouldn't lift it. A hand unplugged the fan and took it away, but the old woman kept covering herself from the air that was no longer blowing, as if floating on the other side of time. In groups of six, the police advanced in semicircles, protected by helmets and visors that covered their chins and necks. Some of them beat people, others fired tear gas.

Look at the ones behind the trees, the doorman said. They're firing on people with rubber bullets.

Run! Run! These wretches are going to kill us! a woman screamed at the television cameramen, as she disappeared into the cloud of smoke.

I sat down in the hotel lobby, defeated. I hadn't found what I'd come to find in Buenos Aires, and now I felt alien to the city as well, alien to the world, alien to myself. What was going on outside suggested a new birth, a beginning of history – or an end – and I didn't understand it, I could only think about Martel's voice, which I'd never heard and might never hear. It was as if the Red Sea was parting before me and the people of Moses, and I, distracted, looked off in another direction. The television repeated fleeting scenes, which lasted only seconds, but when memory bundled all the images up together, that was a tempest.

I think I fell asleep. About eleven at night I was shaken by a vibration of metallic noises that didn't sound like anything I knew. I had the impression that the wind or the rain had gone crazy, and that Buenos Aires was falling to pieces. I'm going to die in this city, I thought. This is the world's last day.

The doorman babbled some hurried phrases of which I only understood a few words. He mentioned a threatening speech by the President of the Republic. We're violent gangs? You hear that, Míster Cogan: violent groups? That's what that jerk said. Enemies of public order, he said. He's more of an enemy of order, I'd say.

The agitation in the streets woke me up. I felt thirsty. I went to the little bathroom by the entrance, washed my face and drank water from my cupped hands.

When I came out, the doorman was bounding up the hotel's deceptive stairway, the loose steps of which had tripped me more that once, while calling me excitedly: Come see this, Míster Cogan! Look at all the people, mamma mía, this is getting out of hand!

We went out on a tiny balcony on the third floor. The waves of humanity were advancing towards the Congress brandishing pot lids and enameled platters, and banging them in a rhythm that never lost a beat, as if they were all reading from the same score. They were chanting an indignant slogan in an angry voice: Out with them all! / Every single one of them!

A young guy with moist black eyes like El Tucumano's was walking at the front of a group of fifteen or twenty people: most of them women with babes in arms or small children hanging on the backs of their necks. One of them shouted up, when she saw us on the balcony: Get down here and be counted! Don't just sit there watching TV!

I felt a pang of nostalgia for my friend, who I hadn't seen since they closed the boarding house on Garay Street, and I had a feeling I'd find him in the effervescence down below. I imagined that he'd hear me, wherever he might be, if I called him with all the desire I was carrying around inside. So I shouted too: I'm coming! I'm coming! Where are you going to meet up? At the Congress, in Plaza de Mayo, everywhere, they answered. We're going everywhere.

I tried to convince the doorman to join the crowd, but he didn't want to leave the hotel undefended and he didn't want to get dressed. He accompanied me to the door, warning me not to talk too much. Your accent really sticks out, he said. Yankee to the core. Be careful. He gave me a white and sky blue striped shirt like the Argentine national soccer team's, and I merged into the crowd.

Everybody now knows what happened during the following days, because the papers talked of nothing else: the victims of a vicious police force, leaving more than thirty people dead, and the pots and pans banging nonstop. I didn't sleep or go back to the hotel. I saw the president flee in a helicopter that rose above a fist-waving crowd, and that same night I saw a man bleed to death on the steps of the Congress building while pushing away with his arms the tragedy coming upon him, going through his pockets and memories to make sure everything was in order, his identity and his past in order. Don't leave us, I shouted at him, hang on, don't leave us, but I knew that it wasn't him I was saying it to. I was saying it to El Tucumano, to Buenos Aires, and to myself, once more.

I walked around the Plaza de Mayo, up Diagonal Norte, where the crowds were smashing in the fronts of the banks, and I even walked as far as the Británico, where I had a coffee and sandwich without any chess players around, or any actors on their way home from the theater. Everything seemed so still, so subdued, and nonetheless no one was sleeping. The clamor of life flowed along the sidewalks and plazas as if the day were beginning. And the day was always beginning whether it was four in the afternoon, midnight or six in the morning.

I'd be lying if I said I thought of Martel while I was wandering from place to place. I thought of Alcira every once in a while, I did think of her, and when I saw the wreckage of flowers strewn around the kiosks on the avenues, I thought of picking up a bouquet for her.

I went back to the hotel on Friday morning, thirty-five hours after going down in search of the demonstrator with the moist eyes – whom I never saw again – and, as I thought it was all over, slept until nightfall. During those days there was a succession of presidents, five in total counting the one I'd seen fleeing in the helicopter, and all of them, except the last, were left alone and abandoned, hiding from the public's fury. The third lasted a week, got as far as sending out Christmas cards and was on the verge of printing a new currency, to replace the eleven or twelve that were circulating out there. He smiled, untiringly, before the tide of misfortune, perhaps because he saw flames where the rest saw only ashes.

The night before that Joker assumed power, a Saturday, I walked to the edge of the river, crossing the tracks of a railway line that no longer existed and defying the dense darkness of the south. An enormous ship, with all its lights on, moved forward on my right, beyond the Fountain of the Nereids, whose impassioned figures had consumed Gabriele D'Annunzio with desire. I had the impression that the ship was slowly cleaving the city's streets, although I knew it was impossible. It moved between the buildings with the rhythm of a ghostly camel, while the night opened its palm and revealed the density of the stars. When the ship disappeared and the darkness returned to close around me, I stretched out on the stone balustrade that rose in front of the riverside bushes and stared at the sky. I discovered that, along with the labyrinth of constellations, between Orion and Taurus, and beyond, between Canopus and the Chameleon, another labyrinth opened up of even more unfathomable empty corridors, spaces clear of celestial bodies, and I understood, or thought I understood, what Bonorino had said to me in the boarding house the night he'd asked for the Prestel book: that the shape of a labyrinth is not in the lines that form it but in the spaces between those lines. Making my way through the vastness of the firmament, I tried to find aisles connecting together the black seams but, as soon as I advanced a tiny bit, a constellation or solitary star would block my path. In the Middle Ages they believed that the figures in the sky mirrored the figures on earth, and so too now, in Buenos Aires, if I walked in one direction history would recede in another, hopes would turn hopeless and the afternoon's joys would become heartaches when night fell. The life of the city was a labyrinth.

I began to suffer blasts of humid heat. The frogs croaked among the reeds of the river. I had to go, because I was being eaten alive by mosquitos.

At noon the next day, the doorman knocked on my door to invite me to sip *maté* and watch the swearing in of the ministers chosen by the Joker.

I would have woken you earlier, Míster Cogan, but I didn't know if I should. An apotheosis, see, we got us a gem of a president now. You wouldn't believe the speech he came out with.

On the television they paraded a couple of political analysts who defined the Joker as a 'whirlwind of work, someone who will do in three months what hasn't been done in ten years.' And so it seemed. When the cameras focused on him, he looked restless, youthful, and he kept repeating: 'Let's see if you've understood me once and for all. I'm the president, got it? Pre-si-dent.'

Wherever he went he was followed by an entourage of functionaries with tape recorders and file folders. On a couple of occasions he asked them to leave him alone to meditate. Through the half-closed door you could see him raise his eyes to the ceiling with his palms together. One of his acolytes caught my attention when I saw him disappearing down one of the corridors in the Presidential Palace. He swayed a little as he walked like El Tucumano. From behind, it could have been him: he was tall, with a strong neck, broad shoulders and thick black hair, but for days I'd been seeing El Tucumano everywhere and didn't know how to get the mirage out of my head.

The Joker's waiting room was full of priests. Some of the Mothers of the Plaza de Mayo were still there, with their white kerchiefs on their heads, after the president had promised them justice in an unexpected interview. I saw a couple of television personalities and the ministers who were preparing to be sworn in. I was starting to get bored when the cameras swung around to a function room where a bust of the Republic could be seen at the front. On the dais set up for the oaths, hundreds of people were trying to make room for themselves and, at the same time, leave a path free for the Joker. They were very stiff in their Sunday suits, not yet believing in the importance that had rained down upon them like sudden manna. They wore ties so flashy they disorientated the cameramen, moccasins with episcopal tassels, silky steam that the electromagnetic television waves could not contain, heavy rings that corrected the beam of the spotlights: such attire could only augur a banquet, although what they were going to devour was nowhere to be seen. I would have enjoyed hearing their conversations, because I would never have the opportunity to see the ostentation of power except in fleeting news bulletins, and what we saw on that afternoon was a power that strutted with neither modesty nor fear, sure of the eternity the Joker had achieved. But the microphones only registered the wave of voices, the redoubled applause for a large crooked crow-like figure, and the cries of the small children who'd been dragged along for the Joker to kiss, in their stiff-fronted shirts and frilly lace skirts.

Not on the dais but in the front row of the audience, among the dignitaries, I caught sight of El Tucumano. The camera gave a quick glimpse of him and I was left doubting whether it was him or not, but a few seconds later, in another shot, I was able to admire his transformation. He had his hair slicked back, was wearing a mustard-colored suit I'd never seen, a tie printed with Bulgarian bacteria and a briefcase between his feet. Black sunglasses, as well. The photographers' flashes sparkled above his pure Hollywood indifference. He's walked along the edge and now he's setting himself up in the center, I thought. Did he owe it to the aleph? I silently sang the praises of the Joker, who was able to produce such miracles. One of the soon to be ministers declared solemnly that the president had gathered together a handful of brilliant men to bring the country back from the abyss. The camera cast a glance at the saviors and left, overwhelmed by the glitter. They were small suns dressed in silks of ivory, mustard, sky blue and lime green. They were all protected by dark sunglasses, perhaps from their own phosphorescence. I sighed. With a quick gesture I severed El Tucumano from my heart forever. Power put him out of my reach, and I didn't want to let myself be blown away by the gale his life had turned into.

I'd called the hospital several times to see how Martel was doing. I did so as soon as I returned from my long wakefulness to the beat of the pots and pans, and then tenaciously every two hours from the very moment I woke up on Friday night. I always got the same answer: no change in the patient's condition.

I thought it sounded discouraging, ominous. What was, for that voice, the dividing line between health and death? A couple of times I dared to ask for Alcira, but I never managed to get them to pass on my messages.

On Sunday I returned to the places where the disturbances had occurred. They still looked like battlegrounds. What am I saying: the memory of the battle hadn't moved. It would remain levitating above the city for who knows how long. The shards of glass, the blood, the steel shutters dented by blows, the lids of the saucepans, the placards wrecked by the police horses and the vile hydrant tanks, the remains of the same clamor everywhere. Out with them all! Out with them all!

The disasters carried on, and so did all of them. The days went by and they stayed on, in the shadow of the Joker.

On the corner of Diagonal Norte and Florida there were two groups with sticks that had not yet sated their eagerness to punish the banks. They wanted to demolish them with their bare hands, brick by brick. I heard a man repeat in despair: This country is finished. If they don't leave, we'll have to go. But where. If only I knew where.

I walked through the Bajo as far as Callao and turned onto Las Heras. The sun was fierce, but I wasn't feeling it anymore. I can't remember ever feeling as lonely as on that afternoon, a solitude that singed me and hurt so much.

I want to see Alcira Villar, I said at the hospital entrance.

Villar Alcira, Villar, we don't have a listing. She's not on staff, the woman at reception informed me. Is she a patient? There are no more visiting hours until tomorrow.

Any news on Martel, Julio Martel? Intensive care unit. Bed fourteen, I think.

I watched her check on the computer, diligent, affable. No change specified, she answered. No change. I'm sure he must be better, or in the same condition.

I went to the café across the street and sat in a corner. Soon it would be New Year, I thought. 2002. A year of arched eyebrows. In the previous three months everything that could happen had happened: the planes crashing into the Twin Towers a few days after my departure from JFK, Buenos Aires aging before my eyes hour by hour, me stupefying myself with the emptiness of never doing anything. Go home. How many times was I going to tell myself? Go home, go home. What was I waiting for? For Martel to die, I thought. I'm the raven croaking over the greatest singer in this moribund nation. I remembered Truman Capote waiting for Perry and Dick, the murderers from *In Cold Blood*, to be hanged, so he could finish his book. I was also flying over the dying embers of a ghost. *Quoth the Raven*, I recited. *Leave my loneliness unbroken!*

Something else, however, could still happen. Alcira came into the café. She sat down by the window, ordered a beer and lit a cigarette. No one was the same during those days, and she wasn't either. I'd imagined her drinking only tea and mineral water, avoiding tobacco. My intuitions crashed to the floor.

She was distracted. She glanced at the news in the paper she had with her, but didn't read it. Discouraged, she pushed the pages away. The people we saw pass by didn't seem overwhelmed but rather incredulous. The country had gone to hell, they all said, but there it was. Can a nation die, by any chance? So many have died and others have come back to breathe among the ashes.

I decided to approach her table. I felt empty. When she looked up at me I noticed in her face the ravages of the last few days. She had lipstick on and a touch of rouge, but the disasters were etched in the circles under her eyes that made her look older. I told her I'd been calling the hospital insistently for news of Martel. I wanted to come and keep her company, I told her, but they wouldn't let me. Over and over again they told me that visitors were forbidden and that the patient's condition was unchanged.

Unchanged? I don't know how to lift his spirits anymore, Bruno. His spleen's distended, he hasn't passed water for days, he's all swollen. Three days ago he seemed to have revived. Around six in the evening he wanted me to sit down beside him. We were talking for an hour, maybe more. He taught me how to memorize numbers and combine them. Three is a bird, thirty-three is two birds, zero three is all the birds in the world. It's an ancient art, he told me. He combined ten or twelve numbers in different ways and then shuffled them backwards. He was speaking in that monotonous rhythm that croupiers use in casinos. As if he were performing. I didn't understand why he was doing it and I didn't want to ask.

Maybe to feel alive. To remember who Martel had once been.

Yes, that must've been it. He wants to get up soon, and sing again. He asked me to book Sabadell for a recital on the Costanera Sur. It's an illusion, you realize. He doesn't even know when he'll be able to stand. What happened on the Costanera? I asked him. That place is a desert now. What do you mean, Alcirita, he answered. Didn't you see it in the paper? I remembered finding a clipping in the pocket of the pants he was wearing when we brought him to the hospital, but I only managed to see the headline. Something about a naked corpse among the reeds.

Has he gone downhill since then? Did you say he's worse?

That very night he took a turn for the worse. He's having trouble breathing. I think they're going to open up his airway. I don't want them to torment him further, but I don't have the right to say so either. I've spent years by Martel's side but I'm still nobody to him.

Tell them how you feel anyway.

What I feel.

Yes, doctors always try to keep people alive, here and everywhere. It's something to do with pride.

I feel that there's no reason for him to die now. Should I tell them? They'll laugh behind my back. I'm not thinking about death. If they want to cut his throat to stick a tube in, how can I explain to them that the voice would disappear, and without the voice, Martel would be another person? He'd let himself die as soon as he found out what had happened. That afternoon, three days ago, I told him about you, I told you, didn't I?

No, you didn't tell me.

I told him that you'd spent months searching for him. Now he knows where I am, he said. So, let him come and talk to me. Bruno can come whenever he wants.

They wouldn't let me see him.

Not now. You have to wait for another resurrection. If you were there all the time you would have seen him come back sometimes so strongly that you'd think: That's it, he's not going to have any more relapses.

If only I could always be at the hospital. But you know it's not up to me.

I looked at her for a long time as if I didn't want to part with her. The tiredness in her eyes kept me there, her smooth skin, her dark hair disordered by the hurricanes of her soul. It seemed to me that those marks of identity summed up those of the human race. Sometimes I stared at her so intensely that Alcira looked away. I would have liked to explain that it wasn't her who attracted me but the lights that Martel had left on her face that I could half make out, the reverberations of the dying voice that were inscribed on her body. Suddenly, Alcira bent over to tie up the laces of her flat, white nurse's shoes. When she sat up she looked at her watch, as if she had just woken up.

Look how late it is, she said. Martel's going to be asking for me.

You've only been here for five minutes, I said. You used to stay longer before.

None of what's happened had happened before. Now we're all walking on broken glass. Five minutes is a whole lifetime.

I watched her go and realized that I had nothing to do away from her. I didn't want to go back to the hotel through bonfires and beggars. At least I now knew Martel had indicated another point on his hypothetical map: the Southern Shore, where I'd been wandering unknowingly on Saturday night. A naked body in the reeds. Perhaps I could find the facts in the archives. I remembered they were all closed and the fires had even reached the doors of one of them. The incident that Martel mentioned, however, probably wasn't so distant. The clipping was still in his pocket. For a moment I hoped that Alcira might let me see it, though I knew her incapable of such disloyalty.

I opened the newspaper she'd left forgotten on the table and I too turned the pages dispiritedly, glancing at the gloomy, bloodstained news. A long article caught my attention, illustrated with photos of barely-dressed children and men among heaps of garbage. 'I turned around and saw they were bullets,' said the defiant headline. There was a more explanatory caption above: 'Fuerte Apache, two days later.' It was a detailed description of the neighborhood where Bonorino and my other neighbors from the boarding house had ended up. It seemed that the first supermarket looters had come from there and now they were holding wakes for their dead.

According to what I read, Fuerte Apache must be a fortress: three ten-story tower blocks joined together on a ten-hectare lot, six blocks west of General Paz Avenue, on the very edge of Buenos Aires. Around the tower blocks they'd been building long three-story houses they called 'strips.' I thought of the librarian moving from one shack to the next with his string of index cards, like a mole. 'At all hours,' the article said, 'music boomed. *Cumbia*, salsa: the kids dance on the mud sidewalks with *litronas* of beer in hand.' I wondered what *litronas* were. Perhaps the young kids' slang was infiltrating the newspapers. 'Fuerte Apache was planned for twenty-two thousand inhabitants but at the end of the year 2000 there were already more than seventy thousand living there. It's impossible to get an accurate figure. Neither census takers nor police would venture through those hallways. Yesterday, at the entrance to the strips, there were ten makeshift funeral chapels. In some of them they were holding wakes for slum-dwellers shot down by the police or supermarket owners during the looting; in others, for victims of stray bullets or fights between rival gangs in the tower blocks.'

At the bottom of the article there was a list of the dead in a succinct inset. I was astonished to discover the name Sesostris Bonorino, municipal employee. A series of memories flashed through my head like a reproach. I remembered the rap the librarian had sung to hand claps, before we'd said goodbye in the boarding house: *In the Fort there's no place to run / Life gets blown to kingdom come / If I live, it's where it smells like dung / If I die, it's a bullet from a stranger's gun*. I should have realized at the time that such an extravagant scene could not have been a coincidence. Bonorino was alerting me to the fact that he'd seen his own finale, that he couldn't avoid it and it didn't matter to him either. Against my clumsy suppositions, it was possible, then, to read the future in *the small iridescent sphere of blinding light*. The aleph existed. It existed. I regretted that the newspaper's epitaph was so unjust. Bonorino had been one of the few privileged people – if not the only one – who, contemplating the aleph, had come face to face with the shape of God.

I had an urge to go to Fuerte Apache to find out what had happened. I couldn't understand how such an innocent being had met such a brutal death. I contained myself. Even if I managed to get into the funeral chapels, there would be no point now. I gradually resigned myself to the idea that the librarian had been able to see everything: my night with El Tucumano in the Hotel Plaza Francia, the treacherous letter I wrote and the useless consequences of my betrayal. I was disconcerted that, even knowing that, he had trusted me with the accounts ledger with the notes for the National Encyclopedia, which was his life's work. What good could it do him that I or anyone else had it? Why had he trusted me?

The only thing that made any sense now was to recover the aleph. If I found it, not only could I see both the foundations of Buenos Aires, the muddy village with its stinking saltery, the revolution of May 1810, the Mazorka's crimes then and again a hundred and forty years later, the arrival of the immigrants, the Centenary celebrations, the Zeppelin flying over the proud city. I could also hear Martel in all the places where he'd sung and know the precise moment when he'd be lucid enough for us to speak.

I got onto the first southbound bus I saw, then walked, almost breathlessly, towards the boarding house on Garay Street. If anyone was still living there, I'd go down to the cellar on whatever pretext I could come up with and lie flat on my back, raising my eyes up toward the nineteenth step. I would see a whole universe in a single point, the torrent of history in an infinitesimal fraction of a second. And if the place was shut up, I'd break down the door or open the old lock. I'd taken the precaution of keeping my keys.

I was prepared for any eventuality, except the one I found. The boarding house had been reduced to rubble. In the space that corresponded to the reception desk sat a sinister-looking digger. The first flight of stairs that used to lead to my room was still standing. At the edge of the street yawned one of those dump trucks used to cart away demolition wreckage. It was late at night by now and the site was unguarded by lights or men. I crawled blindly through the beams and chunks of masonry, knowing that here and there would be holes and if I fell into one I would fracture something fatally. I wanted to get to the cellar no matter what.

I dodged a couple of bricks that fell from the skeleton of

the wall. Even in that desolation with all points of references obliterated, I was sure of being able to find my way around. The counter, I told myself, the remains of the banister, Enriqueta's little cubicle. Ten or twelve steps to the west should be the rectangle through which I'd seen Bonorino's bald head peek out so many times. I jumped over some boards with nails and jagged glass sticking out of them. Then I stumbled into a wooden frame, beyond which opened a pit. The darkness was so dense that I intuited more than I saw. Was it really a pit? I thought I should go down and explore, but I couldn't bring myself to do it. I picked up a piece of rubble, tossed it in, and heard it echo off other stones almost immediately. So it wasn't very deep. Perhaps with the help of a flashlight, I might be able to get down there, no matter how precarious it was. I didn't even have a damn match with me. The moon had gone behind a heavy swell of clouds long ago. It was waxing, almost full. I decided to wait until the sky cleared. I touched the fence and my hands felt a crumpled, sticky piece of paper. I tried to get rid of it but it was stuck to me. It had a thick, rough consistency like a cement bag or cheap cardboard. The fleeting light from the headlights of a passing car enabled me to glimpse what it was. It was one of Bonorino's index cards that had survived the demolition, dust and mechanical diggers. I could make out three letters: I A O. Maybe they didn't mean anything. Maybe, if they hadn't been etched there by chance, they referred to the idea of the Absolute found in *Pistis Sophia*, the sacred books of the Gnostics. I didn't even have time to ponder it. At that instant a break appeared in the clouds and the pit appeared, unmistakable, in front of me. From its dimensions and position I could see that the excavation occupied the same place as the old cellar. Where the nineteen-step staircase had been I could now make out a vertical railing. Just when no one would consider building anything in a crumbling Buenos Aires, my boarding house had been pulled down by bad luck. The aleph, the aleph, I said. I tried to see if there was any trace left. I desolately contemplated the mounds of turned earth, blocks of cement, the indifferent wind. I spent a long time among the ruins, incredulous. A few weeks earlier, when we were saying goodbye in the boarding house, Bonorino had defied me to lie down under the nineteenth step, flat on my back, sure I wouldn't do it. Since he knew everything, he also knew I wouldn't take him up on it. He'd seen the hustle and bustle of the diggers over the rubble of the boarding house, the void, the building that hadn't yet been constructed and the one they'd put up a hundred years later. He'd seen how the small sphere that contained the universe would disappear forever beneath a mountain of garbage. That night in the boarding house I'd wasted my only opportunity. I'd never have another. I screamed, I sat down to cry, I don't even remember what I did anymore. I wandered aimlessly through the Buenos Aires night until, shortly before dawn, I returned to the hotel. I faced, like Borges, intolerable nights of insomnia, and only now can forgetfulness begin to seep in.

The day following this misfortune was New Year's Eve. I got up early, had a quick shower and just a cup of coffee for breakfast. I was in a hurry to get to the hospital. I left a message at the intensive care unit telling Alcira that I'd be waiting for Martel's summons on the steps by the entrance or in the waiting room. I was determined to stay right there. Messages, services, everything seemed to have gone back to normal. The previous night, however, the pots and pans had resounded once again. The umpteenth explosion of popular rage had removed the Joker from power, along with his string of collaborators and ministers. I wondered whether El Tucumano would have returned to his unstable job at Ezeiza, but immediately discarded the idea. A sun that has shone so brightly won't be dragged down.

On the trusty 102 bus there was talk only of the Joker, who had also fled — like the president in the helicopter — from the country in ruins. No one thought it could rise out of such prostration. Those who still had anything to sell refused to do so, because no one knew the value of things. I felt outside of reality now, or rather plunged into that alien reality of the fading life of a tango singer.

I walked through the hospital corridors without being stopped by anyone. When I entered the second-floor waiting room, I recognized the shaven-headed doctor I'd come across a few days before. He was speaking quietly to two old men who were crying with their faces in their hands, ashamed of their grief. As he had done with Alcira, the doctor patted them on the back. When I saw he was going back to work, I caught up to him and asked if I could see Martel.

We have to be careful, he said. Today the patient seems a little down. Are you a relative?

I didn't know how to answer. I'm nobody, I said. Then I hesitantly rectified: I'm a friend of Alcira's.

Let the lady decide, then. The patient has been taking strong painkillers. I assume you've been informed of the latest complication. Advanced necrosis of the liver cells.

Alcira told me that sometimes he recovers for a while and seems to be healthy. One of those times he asked for me. He said I could come in to see him.

When did she say that?

Yesterday, but it was because of something that happened three days ago, or more.

This morning he couldn't breathe. The solution was a tracheotomy, but as soon as he heard that word, he gathered strength from nowhere and shouted that he'd rather die. I think the lady has been awake for days.

It was obvious that Alcira had spoken of the issue with Martel, and that they'd taken the decision together to resist. I said thank you to the doctor. I didn't know what else to say. My singer, then, had reached the end and I would now never have the chance to hear him. Bad luck was pursuing me. Since they'd closed the boarding house on Garay Street, I felt I was arriving late to all of life's opportunities. To distract myself from despondency, I'd spent weeks reading The Count of Monte Cristo in the Laffont edition. Every time I opened the novel I forgot the misfortunes all around. Not this time: this time I felt that nothing could take me away from the curse that circled like a crow and sooner or later would feed on our carrion.

I asked one of the nurses to call Alcira.

I watched her come in five minutes later, carrying a century's worth of tiredness. I'd already noticed, the day before, in the café, that Martel's tragedy had begun to transform her. She moved slowly, as if dragging all the suffering of the human condition in her wake. She asked me:

Can you stay, Bruno? I'm all alone and Julio's in a bad way, I don't know how to raise his spirits. So much struggle, poor thing. Twice he stopped breathing, with such a pained expression, which I never want to see again. A while ago he said: I can't take any more, honey. What do you mean you can't take it? I answered him. And the recitals you've got coming up? I already told Sabadell that the next one is on the Southern Shore. We're not going to stand him up, are we? For a moment, I thought he was going to smile. But he closed his eyes again. He has no strength. You won't leave me alone, will you, Bruno? Please don't leave me. If you stay here reading, waiting for me, I'll feel we're less defenseless. Please.

What was I going to say to her? If she hadn't asked I would have stayed anyway. I offered to buy her something to eat. Who knew how long she'd been there without anything. No, she stopped me. I'm not hungry. The more empty and pure my body is inside, the more awake I'm going to feel. You're not going to believe it but I haven't been home for three days. Three days without a shower. I don't think I've ever gone so long, maybe when I was little. And the strangest thing is I don't feel dirty. I must smell awful, no? I do mind, but at the same time I don't. It's as if all that's happening to me were purifying me, as if I were preparing to not have life.

That torrent of words surprised me. And the confession I wouldn't have thought her capable of. We'd only met a little over two weeks ago. We barely knew anything about each other and, suddenly, we were standing there talking about her body odor. I was taken aback, like so many other times. I know I've said it before, but I can't stop thinking that the true labyrinth of Buenos Aires is its people. So near and at the same time so distant. So similar on the outside and so diverse within. Such reserve, which Borges tried to assert as the essence of the Argentine, and at the same time such shamelessness. Alcira also seemed unfathomable to me. I think she was the only woman I ever wanted to sleep with in my whole life. Not out of curiosity but love. And not for physical love but something deeper: out of need, a craving to contemplate her abyss. And now I didn't know what to do seeing her like this, so desolate. I would have liked to console her, hold her against my chest, but I stood frozen, I dropped my arms and watched her walk away towards Martel's bedside.

I don't know how many hours I stayed in that hospital chair. Some of the time I was on tenterhooks, reading Dumas, attentive to the subtle intrigues of revenge that Monte Cristo was spinning. I knew them already and, nevertheless, the perfect architecture of the tale always surprised me. At dusk, shortly before the poisoning of Valentine de Villefort, I fell asleep. Hunger woke me and I went to buy a sandwich from the café on the corner. They were just about to close and reluctant to serve me. People were in a hurry to get home and the shops' shutters rolled closed almost in unison. The reality of the hospital, however, seemed to belong elsewhere, as if what it contained was too big for its shape. I mean that there were too many emotions in that place than could ever fit in one evening.

I went back to the novel and, when I raised my eyes, everything that I saw out the window was tinted with a golden light. The sun was setting over the city with a magnificence as invincible as on that dawn seen from the Hotel Plaza Francia. With surprise, I noticed that now too I felt an irremediable anguish. I fell asleep again for a while, maybe a couple of hours. I was startled awake by the firecrackers that tore through the night and the tumult of fireworks. I'd never enjoyed new year festivities and more than once, after hearing the crowds count down the seconds on television and watching the invariable annual ball of light drop into its time capsule in Times Square, I'd turned off the bedside lamp and rolled over to go to sleep.

Was it midnight already? No, it couldn't even be ten yet. The nurses were leaving one by one, like the musicians in Joseph Haydn's *Farewell Symphony*, and, in the waiting room, under the fluorescent lights, I was entirely alone. In the distance I heard a sob and the monotony of a prayer. I hadn't even noticed that Alcira had come into the room and was smiling at me. Taking me by the arm, she said:

Martel's waiting for you, Bruno. For a long while now

he's been breathing without problems. The doctor on call says not to get our hopes up, it could be a passing improvement, but I'm sure he's out of danger. He's put so much will into it that he's finally won the fight.

I let her lead me. We went through two swinging doors and entered a large ward, with rows of small rooms separated by panels. Although the place was isolated and in semi-darkness, the sounds of illness, echoing at each step, hurt my ears. Wherever I turned, I saw patients connected to respirators, intravenous drips and cardiac monitors. The last cubicle on the right was Martel's.

I could barely make out his shape among those indirect lights the machines gave off, so my first impression was one I already had in my memory: that of a small man with a short neck and thick black hair who I'd seen, months before, getting into a taxi near Congreso. I don't know why I'd imagined him to look like Gardel. Not a bit: his lips were thick, his nose wide, and in his large dark eyes an anxious expression, of someone running to try to keep up with time. The roots of his hair, which hadn't been dyed since who knows when, were ashen, and here and there were balding patches.

With a slight gesture he pointed me to a chair beside the bed. Up close, the wrinkles formed soft webs in the skin, and his breathing was asthmatic, labored. I had no way of comparing his present condition to that morning when the doctor had found him 'a little down,' but what I saw was enough not to share Alcira's optimism. His body was shutting down faster than the year.

Cogan, he said, with a thread of a voice. I've heard you're writing a book about me.

I didn't want to offend him.

About you, I answered, and about what the tango was like at the beginning of the last century. I heard that there were many of those works in your repertoire and I traveled here to see you. When I arrived, at the end of August, I found out you weren't singing anymore.

What I said seemed to upset him, and he made signs to Alcira to put me right.

Martel never stopped singing, she said obediently. He declined to give recitals for people who didn't understand.

I already knew that. I've been on your trail all these months. I waited in vain one day at noon under the arches in Mataderos, and I found out too late that you'd sung on a corner in Parque Chas. I would have been happy to hear just one line. But there are no traces of you anywhere. No recordings. No videos. Only a few people's memories.

Soon there won't even be that, he said.

His body gave off a chemical smell, and I would have sworn it smelled of blood as well. I didn't want to tire him with direct questions. I felt we had no time for anything else.

More than once I thought your recitals followed some sort of order, I told him. However, I haven't been able to figure out what lies behind that order. I've imagined many possibilities. I even thought the points that you chose were drawing a map of the Buenos Aires that nobody knows.

232

You were right, he said.

He made a barely perceptible sign to Alcira, who was standing at the foot of the bed, with her arms crossed.

It's late, Bruno. Let's let him get some rest.

I thought Martel wanted to raise one of his hands but I realized they were the first parts of him to have died. They were swollen and rigid. I stood up.

Wait, young man, he said. What are you going to remember about me?

I was so surprised by the question that I answered the first thing that came into my head:

Your voice. What I'll most remember is what I've never heard.

Bring your ear close, he said.

I sensed that he was finally going to tell me what I'd waited so long to hear. I sensed that, if only for that moment, my journey was not going to have been in vain. I leaned over gently, or at least I meant to. I have no idea what I did because I was no longer inhabiting myself, and in my place was another body bending toward Martel, trembling.

When I had got close enough, he let the voice loose. In the past it must have been an extremely beautiful voice, unscathed, full as a sphere, because what was left of it, even thinned by illness, had a sweetness that didn't exist in any other voice in this world. He only sang:

Buenos Aires, cuando lejos me vi.

And he stopped. They were the first words to ever have been heard in Argentine cinema. I didn't know what they meant to Martel, but for me they encompassed all that I'd gone to search for, because they were the last words to come out of his mouth. *Buenos Aires, when I'm far away.* I used to think it was his way of saying goodbye to the city. I don't see it like that anymore. I think the city had already dropped him, and he, desperate, was only asking it not to abandon him.

We buried him two days later in Chacarita cemetery. The only thing Alcira could get was a niche on the first floor of a mausoleum where other musicians lay. Although I paid for a funeral announcement in all the newspapers hoping that somebody might come to the funeral chapel, the only ones to sit by his body the whole time were Alcira, Sabadell and me. Before leaving for the cemetery, I hurriedly ordered a spray of camellias, and I still remember walking towards the niche with the spray, not knowing where to put it. Alcira was so heartbroken that nothing mattered to her, but Sabadell complained bitterly about people's ingratitude. I don't know how many times I prevented him from calling El Club del Vino and the Sunderland, before the burial. He did it when I fell asleep in a chair, at three in the morning, but no one answered the phone.

A series of vicissitudes came together to turn Martel's death into a joke of fate. Only days later, when I paid the funeral parlor bill, I saw that the newspapers had announced his death under his real name, Estéfano Esteban Caccace. No one must have remembered that the singer was called that, which explained the solitude of his funeral, but it was too late to repair the damage by then. A long time later, in the summer in Manhattan, I ran into Tano Virgili on Fifth Avenue and we went to have an iced coffee at Starbucks. He told me that he'd seen the announcement and the name had rung a bell from somewhere, but the day of the funeral they were swearing in the fifth president of the Republic, expecting the currency to be devalued and no one could think of anything else.

At the moment Sabadell and I were placing the coffin in the niche, fifteen or twenty wild-looking people burst into the mausoleum, stopping a few steps away from us. Leading the group was a young guy with chipped teeth and a woman with thick makeup plastered on her face waving a little stick. He was carrying a little girl with skeletal legs, who was wearing a lace skirt and a crown of plastic flowers.

Oh my Saint, a miracle, the girl can walk! the woman shouted.

The one with the teeth set the little girl down in front of one of the niches and ordered her:

Walk, Dalmita, so the saint can see you.

He helped her take a step and also shouted:

Have you seen the miracle?

I tried to get close to see who they were venerating, but Alcira stopped me, taking my arm. Since we were waiting for Martel's tomb to be sealed, we couldn't leave at that moment.

They're devotees of Gilda, the laconic Sabadell explained. That woman died seven or eight years ago in a car accident. Her *cumbias* weren't very popular when she was alive, but look at her now.

I would have liked to ask her devotees to be quiet. I realized it would have been useless. A huge woman, with a tower of blonde hair and lips broadened with purple lipstick, took something that looked like a deodorant out of her purse and, holding it like a microphone, urged the faithful:

Come on girls, everyone sing to our Gilda!

She then embarked on an out-of-tune *cumbia*, which began: *I don't regret this looove / though it cost me my heeeart.* The singing went on for five interminable minutes. Long before the end, they accompanied the chorus with hand clapping, until one of the devotees – or whatever they were – shouted: Grand Wild Lady!

We left fifteen minutes later with a greater desolation than the one we'd arrived with, feeling guilty for leaving Martel in an eternity so saturated with hostile music.

I was worried about Alcira being alone and I invited her to meet me that same evening, at seven, in the Café La Paz. She arrived punctually, with that strange striking beauty that obliged eyes to turn, as if the tempest of the last month hadn't touched her. I helped her to pour out her heart telling me how she'd fallen in love with Martel the first time she heard him sing in El Rufián Melancólico, and how she gradually overcame the resistance he put up, the fear of revealing his sickly, helpless body. He was solitary and surly, she told me, and it took him months to trust her. When she finally managed it, Martel began to develop an increasingly intense dependency. He'd sometimes call her in the middle of the night to tell her his dreams, then he taught her how to give him injections in his almost invisible, excessively damaged veins, and finally wouldn't let her leave his side and tormented her with jealous scenes. They ended up living together in the flat Alcira rented on Rincón Street, near Congreso. The house Martel had shared with his mother in Villa Urquiza was falling to pieces and they had to sell it for less than the memories were worth.

One conversation led to another, and now I don't remember if it was that day or the next when Alcira started to tell me in detail about Martel's solitary recitals. She knew from the start why he chose each one of the sites, and even suggested some which he rejected because they didn't fit exactly into his map.

A year before I arrived in Buenos Aires he'd sung on the corner of Paseo Colón and Garay Street, just three blocks from the boarding house. A few metal silhouettes clinging to a bridge were the only signs of the pit of torment that, during the dictatorship, was known as the Club Atlético. When they were going to demolish it to build the Ezeiza motorway, Martel managed to see the skeleton of the lion's den where hundreds of prisoners had died, whether from the tortures applied on enormous metal tables, a few steps from the cages, or because they'd been hung on hooks until they bled to death.

He sang in the early hours of a summer morning in front of the Jewish community center on Pasteur Street, where in July 1994 a truck full of explosives blew up, destroying the building and killing eighty people. More than once it was thought the killers were within reach of justice and it was even said that the Iranian Embassy had protected them, but as soon as the investigation advanced a tiny bit insuperable obstacles arose. Months after Martel's recital, the *New York Times* published the news on the front page that the then president of Argentina had received, perhaps, ten million dollars so the crime would go unpunished. If it was true, that would explain everything.

He also sang on the corner of Carlos Pellegrini and Arenales, where a paramilitary gang murdered the politician Rodolfo Ortega Peña in July 1974, shooting him from inside a light green Ford Fairlane that belonged to Perón's astrologer's fleet. Martel had passed when the body was still lying on the sidewalk, the blood flowing toward the street and a woman with her lips perforated by a bullet begging the dead man please not to die. He didn't want to sing a tango in that spot, Alcira told me. The only thing he intoned was a long lament, an *ay* that lasted until the sun set. Then he remained *silent like a child beneath the fat vultures*.

And he sang – but this was before all the rest – in front of the old metal works on Vasena, in San Cristóbal, where thirty striking workers were murdered by the police during uprisings of 1919 still known as the Tragic Week. Maybe he would also have sung for the dead of the fatal December in which he died, but no one told him what was happening.

Halfway through January 2002, on one of the worst days of the summer, when the people seemed to be getting used to the incessant disgrace, Alcira told me that, just before the fateful recital in Parque Chas, Martel had read the story of a crime committed between 1978 and 1979, and had kept the clipping with the intention of giving one of his solitary concerts there too. The news, censured by the papers of the day, spoke of a corpse washed up among the reeds on the Southern Shore, near the pergola of the old municipal swimming beach, with the fingers burned, the face disfigured and no identifiable marks. Thanks to the spontaneous confession of a corvette pilot it became known that the dead man had been thrown into the waters of the Río de la Plata alive, and that his body, carried by contrary current, had resisted sinking, being eaten by fish or being dragged, like so many others, to the shores of Uruguay. The clipping said that the dead man had been arrested with Rúben, Magic Eye or Felipe Andrade Pérez. Martel was desperate to sing to that unfortunate man, and if he resisted death for so long, Alcira told me, it was only in the hope of getting to the pergola at the river's edge.

The map, then, was simpler than I'd imagined. It didn't draw any alchemic figure or hide the name of God or repeat phrases from the Kabbalah, but followed, by chance, the itinerary of crimes committed with impunity in the city of Buenos Aires. It was a list that contained an infinite number of names and that was what had most attracted Martel, because it served as an incantation against cruelty and injustice, which were also infinite.

That atrociously hot day I told Alcira that I'd booked my plane ticket to return to New York at the end of the month, and I asked her if she wouldn't like to come with me. I didn't know how two of us could live on the meager stipend I got from student grants, but I was sure I wanted her by my side, no matter what. A woman who had loved

Martel the way she had was capable of enlightening anyone's life, even one as grey as mine. She held my hands, she thanked me with a gentleness that still hurts, and answered no. What would become of me in a country I have nothing to do with? I don't even know how to speak English.

Live with me, I said, stupidly.

You have many years of light ahead of you, Bruno. And around me is only darkness. It wouldn't be good to mix things.

She began to stand up but I begged her to stay a moment longer. I didn't want to return to the unknown night. I didn't know how to say what I finally said:

I still have one question. I've been meaning to ask you for a long time, but you probably don't even know the answer.

I confessed my betrayal of Bonorino, told her about his death in Fuerte Apache and revealed all that I knew about the aleph. I wanted to understand, I said, why the librarian left the notebook that was also his whole life in my hands.

Because you weren't going to betray him again.

It can't be just that. There's something else.

Because human beings, as insignificant as we are, always try to live on. Somehow or other, we want to defeat death, find some form of eternity. Bonorino didn't have friends. You were all that was left to him. He knew, sooner or later, you'd put his name in a book.

I'm going to feel lost without you, I said. I'll feel less lost if we write every once in a while.

I don't want to write anything except my memories of Martel, she answered without looking at me.

So this is the end.

Why? There is no end. How can you know when the end is?

I went to the washroom and when I came back she was gone.

I called her ten or twenty times right up to the very afternoon of my departure. She never answered. The first day I heard an impersonal message that only repeated her phone number. After that the phone rang and rang in the void.

All the flights to New York left at night, so I didn't take my leave of the Buenos Aires I'd imagined but of the reverberation of its lights. Before veering north, the plane lifted over the river and skirted the edge of the city. It was immense and flat and I don't know how many minutes it took to cross. I'd so often dreamed of the layout as seen from above that the reality disconcerted me. I imagined it would resemble the palace of Knossos or the rectangular mosaic of Sousse with the warning inscribed: *Hic inclusus vitam perdit.* Whoever is shut in here will lose his life.

It was a labyrinth, just as I had supposed, and Alcira had got caught in one of its cul-de-sacs. The night allowed me to observe that, just as Bonorino had conjectured, the true labyrinth was not marked out by the lights, where there were only paths that led nowhere, but by the lines of darkness, which indicated where the people lived. A Baudelaire poem, 'The Beacons,' came into my head: *Ces malédictions, ces blasphèmes, ces plaintes, / Ces extases, ces cris, ces pleurs, ces Te Deum, / Sont un écho redit par mille labyrinthes. These curses,*

these blasphemies, these lamentations, / These Te Deums, these
ecstasies, these cries, these tears, / Are an echo repeated by a thousand
labyrinths. I could no longer hear all those voices and the
labyrinth had disappeared into the night. But I kept repeating
the poem until I fell asleep.

A few weeks after arriving back in Manhattan, I began to
receive urgent letters from the Fulbright Foundation, de-
manding a report on the use I'd made of the grant. I tried to
explain it in formal documents that I drafted and then tore
to shreds, until I gave up. I trusted that sooner or later they'd
give up on my silence.

One afternoon in May I left my house and walked
distractedly down Broadway. I stopped in at Tower Records with the impossible hope of finding a recording of
Martel. I'd already tried before. The helpful employees
looked him up on their computers and even called experts
on South American music on the phone. No one had ever
heard of him, there wasn't even the slightest mention of him
in any anthology. I knew all this, of course, but I still refused
to believe it.

I strayed over toward University Place and, as I passed the
university bookstore, I remembered that I wanted to buy
Walter Benjamin's *Arcades Project.* The volume cost more
than forty dollars and I'd been resisting it for weeks, but that
day I let fate decide for me. I was whiling away the time
looking through the philosophy section and I found a copy
of Richard Foley's *Intellectual Trust.* People will say that
none of this is important and maybe it's not, but I'd rather
not overlook the slightest detail. I picked up the Benjamin

again and opened it at random, in a section called 'Theory of Progress' I read this line: 'Knowledge comes only in lightning flashes. The text is the long roll of thunder that follows.' The phrase reminded me of Buenos Aires, which had been a revelation to me but whose rolls of thunder, now, were impossible to turn into words.

When I left with the Benjamin in my hand, I ran into Foley himself. I barely know him, but he's the Dean of Arts and Sciences of my university and I always greet him respectfully. He, nevertheless, knew of my trip to Buenos Aires. He asked me how the experience had been. I responded clumsily, tripping over my words. I told him about the bad times I'd witnessed, the five presidents in the space of ten days, and mentioned in passing that the tango singer who I wanted to write about had died the very night I saw him for the first time.

Don't let that get you down, Bruno, Foley said. What's lost on one side can sometimes be recovered on another. In July, I was in Buenos Aires for ten days. I didn't go looking for any singer but I found an extraordinary one. He was singing century-old tangos in the Club del Vino. Maybe you know him. He's called Jaime Taurel. He's got a moving, clear voice, so vivid you feel if you stretched out your hand you could touch it. When I left, people were saying he was better than Gardel. You should go back, just to hear him.

That night I couldn't sleep. When dawn began to break, I sat down at the computer and wrote the first few pages of this book.

Except for Jean Franco and Richard Foley, all the characters in this novel are imaginary, even those who seem real.

NOTES

11 *Milongas*: Tango clubs or salons. A milonga is also an early twentieth-century Argentinian musical form, a precursor of the tango.

13 *El Rufián Melancólico* (The Melancholy Pimp): the bookstore is named after a character from Roberto Arlt's 1929 novel *The Seven Madmen*

14 *Porteños*: Natives of Buenos Aires; literally, people from the port.

31 Unitarians: Progressive, liberal opponents of Juan Manuel de Rosas (1793–1877, provincial cattle baron who went on to become a so-called Federalist governor of Buenos Aires between 1829–32 and 1835–52, gradually accumulating national powers), hundreds of whom were killed, and often tortured, by the Mazorca, his secret police.

Rosas' daughter, Manuelita, served as his first lady after her mother's death in 1838 and didn't marry until the age of 36, in 1852, after he was overthrown but escaped in disguise to a British warship. He and his daughter were granted asylum in England and he spent the rest of his life on a farm near Southampton, where he ripped out 'two thousand enormous trees' in an attempt to recreate the landscape of the pampas.

31 Revolution of the Park: Uprising in 1890 leading to a bloody confrontation between revolutionaries and armed government forces.

31 Tragic Week: Violent clashes in the second week of January 1919 between striking workers and a repressive police force backed up by paramilitary vigilantes who attacked unions, synagogues, leftist and anarchist groups leaving 700 people dead and 3,000 injured.

31/2 *Plaza de Mayo*: Buenos Aires' main public square, overlooked by the Cathedral, National Bank and the *Casa Rosada* or Presidential Palace. In the 1950s supporters of Eva and Juan Perón, known as *descamisados* – shirtless ones – would gather here in huge crowds. In

1955 the military bombed the plaza, killing over 200, in an attempt to overthrow Perón; they succeeded in doing so in December of the same year.

Every Thursday the Mothers of the Plaza de Mayo still march to protest the impunity of the military that was behind the disappearance of their loved ones during the most recent dictatorship (1976–1982).

Large protests in the Plaza de Mayo in December 2001 led to the resignation of Fernando de la Rúa, and several subsequent presidents.

32 Pedro Henríquez Ureña (1884–1946): Dominican writer and professor who moved to Argentina in 1924 and lived there till his death – on a train pulling out of Constitución Station at midday – on the 11th of May, 1946. (See 'The Dream of Pedro Henríquez Ureña' by Jorge Luis Borges, 1972)

32 Di Tella Institute (*Instituto Torcuato di Tella*): Important Buenos Aires art gallery; hosted influential exhibitions in the 1960s of work by Luis Felipe Noé (1933–), Ernesto Deira (1928–86) and Jorge de la Vega (1930–71), collectively known as the *Otra Figuracion* group.

32 Onganía, General Juan Carlos: Military dictator 1966-1969. Forbade a 1968 performance of Bach's *Magnificat* at the Di Tella Institute by way of a decree against excessive noise.

41 *Camino Negro*: Formerly a notoriously dangerous, narrow, poorly lit highway through the poor southern suburbs, now in ruins.

127 Julio Jorge Nelson: Tango lyricist and host of radio programs devoted almost exclusively to Carlos Gardel. Since Gardel left no heirs and Nelson made so much money from the reflected glory he began to be referred to ironically as *la Viuda de Gardel* or Gardel's Widow.

138 *Adán Buenosayres*: Experimental quest novel by Leopoldo Marechal, published in 1948.

139 José Hernández: Author of 'Martín Fierro', epic poem published in 1872 about a persecuted *gaucho*.

140 *Matraca*: wooden noisemaker especially popular during Carnival.

154 Pibe Cabeza: Nickname of Rogelio Gordillo (1910–1937) leader of heavily armed criminal gang. After topping the most wanted list, he died in a shoot-out with police in Mataderos on February 9th 1937.

222 Centenary celebrations: Celebrations of the revolution of 1810 when Spanish rule ended in Argentina.

A NOTE ON THE AUTHOR AND TRANSLATOR

Tomás Eloy Martínez was born in Argentina in 1934.
During the military dictatorship, he lived in exile
in Venezuela, where he wrote his first three books, all
of which were republished in Argentina in 1983, in
the first months of democracy. He is currently a
professor and director of the Latin American Studies
Program at Rutgers University. He was shortlisted for
the 2005 International Man Booker Prize.

Anne McLean has translated Latin American and
Spanish novels, short stories, memoirs and other
writings by authors including Carmen Martín Gaite,
Ignacio Padilla, Orlando González Esteva, Javier Cercas
and Julio Cortázar. She was awarded the Premio
Valle Inclan for Literary Translation and the
Independent Foreign Fiction Prize in 2004 for her
translation of Javier Cercas' *Soldiers of Salamis*.

A NOTE ON THE TYPE

The text of this book is set in Bembo. This type was first used in 1495 by the Venetian printer Aldus Manutius for Cardinal Bembo's *De Aetna*, and was cut for Manutius by Francesco Griffo. It was one of the types used by Claude Garamond (1480–1561) as a model for his Romain de L'Université, and so it was the forerunner of what became standard European type for the following two centuries. Its modern form follows the original types and was designed for Monotype in 1929.